Dear Daughter

KASSANDRA GARRISON

ISBN: 979-8-9861247-2-8 (E-Book)

ISBN: 979-8-9861247-3-5 (Paperback)

Any references to historical events, real people, or real places are used fictitiously. Names, characters, and places are products of the author's imagination.

Front cover photo taken by Kelli Williams Photography.

Dear Nora,

My sweet, sassy, smart daughter,

Never forget the amazing love God has for you. Lean on Him and search for Him in both the hills and valleys of life.

You will forever be my greatest accomplishment. Even when I am gone, my love will forever exist in you and in the words on these pages.

I love you, Nora Elaine.

My life, this book… it all started with you.

Chapter One

Olivia blinked heavy eyes against flickers of darkness. Above her, the hospital lights of Bailey Memorial Hospital's labor and delivery unit flashed brightly as chills rolled up her spine, her consciousness fading with each passing second. The warm presence of her newborn daughter on her chest was a stark contrast to her cold body.

In her struggle to stay awake, Olivia could see the tiny body lying on her chest. Ten little fingers raised in the air as if in protest of their unfamiliar environment. Tiny murmurs and sudden outbursts came from her wiggling daughter.

Her husband, Greyson, stood next to the bed glancing back and forth between the doctor and his wife, worry clouding his normally warm eyes. Wavy strands of dark hair tumbled onto his forehead over his furrowed eyebrows.

The voice of the doctor sounded distant as he began giving orders to the nurses surrounding the bed, "She's losing too much blood. We need to get her to surgery right away to find the cause. Nurse, take the baby from her chest…"

In the last remaining seconds of awareness, Olivia witnessed her daughter being taken from her and heard the sound of her tiny cries as the nurse carried her across the room to the infant warmer. Though Olivia tried to object, there was no energy left in her body.

Her husband was running his hands through his chocolate brown hair in panic as his attention darted between his wife and daughter. As she looked into his desperate caramel brown eyes, Olivia could hear him calling out to her, "Liv! Olivia! Stay awake, baby. Liv, please. No, no, no."

His words echoed in her ears as her head fell back onto the pillow. Even in the dark recesses of her mind, she could still see his eyes, still hear their daughter crying as he yelled her name.

Suddenly, there was nothing. No sounds. No vision. Only darkness and her thoughts.

Is this what dying feels like? I expected heaven to be brighter than this and maybe paved in gold. This is just darkness. Uh oh... unless I ended up in hell. Oh, no. God, can you hear me?!? I'm not ready to die. I want to hold my daughter in my arms and point out all the ways she's like her daddy. I want Greyson. His warmth, his laugh, his scent. Please let me go back.

Olivia listened for a reply to no avail, her voice swallowed in the darkness.

If our daughter was left with one parent, Grey would be her best option. And he'd have his parents to help him. Before I went into labor, we talked about if something went wrong. I just wish...

Her thoughts were interrupted with a distant soft glow. As it pulsated, the warmth of its light enveloped Olivia, the lack of nothingness a comfort to her. Shapes and colors began to appear around her. The room she occupied and its contents became clearer with each passing moment.

"Olivia, wake up and get ready for school! You don't want to make your father late for work."

Mom?

Olivia studied her surroundings, realizing she was no longer in the hospital. Instead, she found herself an hour away in her hometown of Joliet, Indiana.

She was in her childhood room, the white dresser with hand-painted flowers across the drawers and the purple comforter on her bed a familiar sight. Swiftly, the blankets were thrown from her legs and she began digging through her closet and dresser for clothes to wear.

Wait. What am I doing? Why can't I control my body? I don't need to get dressed for school. I need to go back to my family.

Her little hands stayed busy, pulling a purple shirt featuring butterflies over her head and adjusting her favorite pair of pants. When she straightened in front of the dresser mirror, the face staring back at her wasn't the Olivia who had aged twenty-four years and had just given birth.

It was eight-year-old Olivia with a small round face and large hazel eyes still filled with so much hope and naivety. Her dark brown hair fell just around her shoulders in waves still rumpled from her pillow.

God, what's going on? I can't control my actions and I'm a kid living with my mom. Please, I can't live under the same roof as her again.

Hurriedly, Olivia slipped into a pair of shoes from beside her bed and rushed through her bedroom door. The sound of small feet pattering down the hall followed her into the kitchen where her mother stood by the stove.

In one hand, she held a wooden spoon while the other sat against her hip. The smell of scrambled eggs filled the air as she turned with the steaming pan in her hand, shoveling a mound of eggs onto three plates on the kitchen table.

Olivia's mother was a beautiful woman. Her almond-shaped brown eyes were bordered by high cheekbones and wavy, dark auburn hair, its soft tendrils falling around her face and neck. She was slim with delicate curves running from her shoulders to her hips.

Yet, it wasn't the outside of her mother which Olivia suffered to endure but what was found on the inside: her bitter attitude toward the world, her incessant nagging when things weren't done exactly as she preferred, and her resentful behavior toward her husband and young daughter.

Her mother's eyes locked on Olivia as she walked into the kitchen, scrutinizing her appearance down to every minor detail. From countless mornings when her mother found a flaw, Olivia knew she would have to change something about herself. As her mother's mouth opened, Olivia climbed into her chair at the breakfast table, flinching inwardly at the approaching criticism.

"Olivia Larson, would it kill you to run a brush through your hair? My goodness, it looks like a bird nested in those tangles. And put on different shoes. I don't know what you were thinking by putting brown shoes with those black pants. Really, Olivia, I would think you'd know better by now. Every morning, I have to go through this with you…"

Her mother's voice faded as Olivia sulked back to her bedroom, grabbing the brush on her dresser and running it through her hair. Every criticism her mother spit at her day after day had already started taking a toll on her juvenile mind.

No wonder I have low self-esteem. That woman never gave me a break. Nothing was ever good enough. I was never good enough.

Olivia watched as her eight-year-old self put the brush back in its place on her dresser and looked in the reflection. Tears began to form in the corners of her eyes, her reflection holding no comfort for her, only flaws.

Back at the breakfast table with a different pair of shoes on her feet, she ate her eggs at the pace her mother demanded. If she was too slow, she would be late. If she was too fast, her mother would warn her about gaining weight.

The back door clattered as the sound of her father's boots hit the floor. Olivia looked up excitedly only to receive a scowl from her mother, warning her not to leave her breakfast.

"Daddy!"

Wow. I forgot how excited I used to get when my dad was around.

"Hey, baby girl. How did you sleep?" Her father's hazel eyes, identical to her own, twinkled with warmth and love as he patted her shoulder and kissed the top of her head.

Olivia's small feet kicked eagerly under her chair as she conversed with her father, "Good. I had that dream about the dinosaurs again."

"Again? Isn't that the third time this week?"

He chuckled as he buttered his toast. Her mother abruptly stood up from the table holding her half-eaten plate. She rolled her eyes in irritation, most likely making a mental note to remind her husband about his cholesterol later.

"Yeah. But this time, they weren't cooking in the kitchen, they were wearing clothes and walking down the street past our house."

Olivia and her father laughed together over their breakfast as her mother began scrubbing a skillet in the sink, scouring unnecessarily hard for the task at hand.

She never was happy, was she? There's always something to be done when nothing is good enough.

Eight-year-old Olivia placed her plate in the sink after rinsing it, setting the fork on top of the dish as her mother required. She grabbed the sack lunch prepared for her from the counter and ran out the back door after her father, his truck keys jingling in hand.

She climbed into the passenger seat and buckled up, her father glancing over to make sure she was settled before pulling out of the driveway. He was a handsome man with dark features, a slim build, and a relaxed personality. Perhaps too relaxed at times.

"Dad?"

"Yes, Olivia?"

"Why is Mommy so mean all the time?"

Olivia watched as her father repositioned himself in his seat, unsure how to answer his daughter's question. His dark brows were furrowed and his lips pursed.

"Why do you say that, baby?"

"Because she's always saying mean things about how I look or what I do. And she gives me mean looks all the time. Why doesn't she like me, Daddy?"

By the time Olivia finished explaining her question, her father pulled into the parking lot of her grade school.

The town of Joliet was quite small with only one elementary school located just down the road from their house. He unbuckled and turned toward his daughter, running his rough worker hand over hers.

"Mommy loves you. She just wants what's best for you. She's not trying to be mean. She's trying to help you."

Yeah, if incessant nagging, degrading, and yelling were helping.

Olivia nodded her head slowly, unpersuaded of his statement, and waited for her father to open her truck door from outside. She grabbed his hand as she jumped down onto the pavement, his calluses and scars contrasting her soft skin. He worked in the garage most nights after dinner, likely trying to avoid her mother as much as possible.

"Have fun at school, sweetheart. I'll pick you up at three. I love you."

"Love you, Daddy."

As if her body ran away without her soul, Olivia watched as her younger self departed for school, leaving her alone with her father in the parking lot. She witnessed her father's smile turn into a frown, his hand running over his face in frustration when his eight-year-old daughter could no longer see him. He pulled his phone from his pocket, dialed a number, and waited for an answer.

"Yeah, we need to talk about your attitude."

There was a brief pause as an irritated female voice replied from the other end.

"I've witnessed your behavior get worse and worse. Our daughter just asked why her mother is so mean. She's eight years old, Renee! No, I won't apologize. I'm sick of this. I don't know what will make you happy…"

The memory faded slowly to darkness again with the silhouette of her dad disappearing last. Olivia was once again alone with her thoughts.

I didn't know Dad called Mom that day. That explains why she gave everyone the silent treatment after school, a glass of wine her only company. There was no winning with her. She was right and if you tried to prove otherwise, she played the victim. It's no wonder my dad stopped trying.

As a soft, warm light began returning to Olivia's vision, she braced herself for yet another memory from a past she had attempted to forget.

Chapter Two

"Now, once we get these green beans snapped, we'll go inside and cook them for lunch. Does that sound good?"

Grandma?

At the sound of her grandmother's voice, Olivia's heart skipped a beat. It had been nearly a decade since she had seen her grandmother. Too long.

"Yes, ma'am." Olivia's slightly matured voice sounded foreign to her now, the eight-year-old version of herself left in the previous memory. Her vision cleared as the scene continued to unfold.

Grandma Vi sat next to Olivia on her grandmother's shady porch overlooking the back yard. To their left was a large garden with vegetables and fruits planted in neat, straight rows. On the opposite side of the yard was a large Rose of Sharon bush in full bloom. Its large purple flowers danced in the warm summer breeze.

Vi's dark hair with strands of silver was pulled back in a simple bun. She had a petite frame and sharp eyes which could read anyone like a book.

"That's my girl. How's your mama and daddy doing?"

Olivia's happy demeanor vanished at the mention of her home life. Her grandmother, Vi, having the gift of discernment, furrowed her dark brow at her now somber grandchild.

"They still fighting a lot, sugar?"

With a nod of the head, Olivia confirmed her grandmother's suspicions, tightening the lips of the elder into a firm line of disappointment.

"You want to talk about it? Remember, you can tell Grandma anything."

I really could. I miss that.

Vi continued to snap off the ends of green beans they had just harvested from her garden, placing the ends in a plastic bag next to her feet and the beans in a bowl between the two of them.

Olivia kept her head down and opened her mouth to speak but no words came out. Hot tears stung her eyes before tumbling down her cheeks. Her grandmother dropped the green beans in her hands and wrapped her arms around the small, vulnerable adolescent.

"Shh, honey. It's okay. I got you."

Her grandmother rocked as she hummed an old hymn under her breath. After several tears were shed, Olivia needed to relieve the heaviness in her chest caused by her unstable home life.

Her voice was raspy from crying as she poured her heart out to her grandmother, "They fight all the time. It's all night and in the morning, too. Mom will start fights when I'm in the room but Dad will stay quiet until I'm gone."

"What are they fighting about?"

"Everything. Mom isn't happy and Dad doesn't know what to do about it. She gets angry about everything. He goes out to the garage a lot."

"Yes, my son was never one for bickering. He gets his distaste for drama from me."

Her throaty chuckle vibrated against Olivia's arm as she continued to alleviate some of the pain which had built up.

"The night of my birthday a month ago, I heard my mom say she never wanted me. She said she had wasted the last twelve years of her life."

Olivia's grandmother stiffened at her granddaughter's confession, immediately dropping her arms and standing up. She knelt on the step in front of Olivia and pulled the young girl's chin up gently with her hand.

"Now, you listen to me, child. You are not unwanted. God created you with a special purpose in mind. You will do great things in this life. I love you. Your daddy loves you. But, most importantly, and listen to me good now: God loves you. His love is the only love you will ever need. Do you hear me?"

Her grandmother's eyes were glossy yet stern as she continued to look into Olivia's eyes. With an unpersuaded nod from Olivia, her grandmother stood up and brushed the dust from her knees. Vi grabbed the bowl of green beans from its place on the porch and started for the back door.

"Come on, sweetheart. Let's make lunch. I'm starving."

And just like that, Olivia put aside her raw emotions and shared the afternoon with her grandma as she had done so many times before.

Although Olivia's mother did not allow her to attend church with Vi, she was permitted to spend every Sunday afternoon with her. They would cook lunch, tend the garden, sing hymns, and walk down the street to the park.

Olivia's grandmother was the only person in whom she could confide about her home life. Her friends at school were unaware of the turmoil present in her life, assuming, as anyone would, that she had parents who loved one another and didn't spend the lion's share of their time fighting.

Standing beside her grandmother at the stove in her kitchen, Olivia watched as she dropped green beans by the handful into a simmering pot of water. The smell of pork chops and mashed potatoes filled the air as they prepared the last dish.

"Olivia, have I ever told you the entire story about your parents?"

"No, ma'am. They told me they met in grade school."

Olivia continued to watch as her grandmother drained the water from the pot into the nearby sink. She returned the pot to the stove, adding a dab of butter and stirring until it coated the green beans.

"Yes, that's right. They were best friends since about your age. Her parents and I were good friends before they moved down to Florida. We spent a lot of time together. Your parents were practically raised together. Well, once they got into high school, they must have realized it was much more than a friendship they shared.

I warned Ellis, your father, about getting too involved with romance in high school. They were both good kids, went to church every Sunday with me, got good grades in school… but then, before I knew it, she was pregnant. It was near the end of their senior year of high school."

Olivia watched with wide eyes as her grandmother recounted a part of her parents' story she had never before heard. Her grandma turned off the stove burner and began dishing food onto two separate plates, placing them on the table as she continued the story.

"My boy was raised to be responsible for his actions so he proposed to your mother and they married at the courthouse before you were born. They wanted to marry at the church but because they were teenagers with a child out of wedlock, they were turned away at the door."

"But, Grandma, why would the church do that?"

Her grandmother took a bite of steaming mashed potatoes and swallowed before continuing the story.

"Sometimes Christians are so obsessed with their reputations, personal agendas, and church politics that they forget what Christianity is all about: loving God and loving others. Christianity isn't for perfect people; it's for sinners. You don't go to church when you've got your life straightened up. You go there to heal, to repent, and to be completed by a perfect God and His unconditional love."

"Why didn't you tell them that, Grandma?"

"I did, sweetheart. They just didn't listen. Believe me, I did everything in my power to help your parents. Even when her parents moved away and failed to keep in touch, I was there for Renee and Ellis. After that, your mother stayed home to take care of you while your father went to school and got a job at the local factory to support his family."

"So, that's why Mom doesn't want me. She didn't want to get pregnant in the first place and be forced to give up her life to take care of me."

"There are no mistakes, child. God created you for a reason just like He created your daddy and mama. Before He created the birds of the sky and the fish in the sea, He knew your story. From beginning to end."

I miss her so much.

That evening when her grandmother dropped Olivia off at home, she told her son to get his wife and come out on the front porch. Ellis's eyebrows raised. He knew a scolding was in his near future and flinched when he was sent to retrieve his wife.

"I will see you next weekend, Olivia. I love you, sweetheart. Now go inside and get ready for bed."

"Yes, Grandma. I love you, too."

As Olivia stood at the front door, Ellis held it open and waited for her and her mother to step over the threshold. Her mother seemed extremely irritated at the disruption, folding her arms over her chest when she came to a stop on the porch and glared down at her mother-in-law.

Twelve-year-old Olivia prepared for bed while her older version stayed behind to witness the conversation she had once been kept from hearing.

"Lose the attitude, Renee. I'm here to help. There's something I need to say…"

"Don't give me your holier-than-thou speech again, Vi. What do you want?

Her grandmother's tone was short and unapologetic, "It's not just what I want. It's what that child needs."

Olivia's mother was not soft when it came to confrontation as she was usually the one starting the fight, "You're not going to stand there and tell me what MY child needs."

"She needs parents who don't fight all day long and a mother who doesn't chastise her every move. Renee, your bitter attitude is detrimental to this entire household: to your daughter, your husband, and yourself."

"We are doing just fine. Thanks for stopping by."

Renee smirked at her mother-in-law before turning and walking back inside, grabbing the wine glass she had set down just a moment ago. Once out of sight, Vi turned toward her son who had chosen to remain quiet during the entire argument.

"And what do you have to say for yourself, Ellis? Is this what you do in your home, too? Just stand there while she destroys everything in her path? I raised you better than that."

"Mom, I don't know what to do anymore. She's out of control. No matter what I say or do, it's wrong. I never wanted Olivia to live in a broken household..."

His voice was strained as he glanced back at his home toward the window of Olivia's bedroom.

"I know growing up without your daddy was hard, Ellis..."

"He died in a car crash when I was three, Mom. He couldn't help that. But *I* have the choice to keep my family together. And I'm trying..."

"I know, honey. You'll never hear me advocate for divorce before counseling. Whatever you do, son, you need to get your house in order. Take care of my girl. I'll pick her up next Sunday after church."

Olivia's father nodded as his mother patted him on the arm and walked back to her car, turning the engine over before pulling off in the direction of her home.

This is the conversation that made my parents go to marriage counseling. Too bad it only made things worse. My mom grew more resentful, claiming counseling was my dad's way of blaming her.

This is only going to escalate even more. God, why can't I just go back to my family? Why do I have to relive these moments? I just want to see Grey.

And with that, another memory was returned to the pitch-black abyss of her mind before the next began right on cue.

Chapter Three

"Thanks to you, I'm stuck in this tiny town where everyone knows my business. I wish I never met you, Ellis. You ruined my life."

Olivia could hear her mother's voice from her bedroom where she lay on her bed, a pillow pressed around her ears to soften the disruption outside her door.

She was fifteen now, too young to drive away from the fighting yet old enough to dream of doing so. It didn't matter that it was Christmas Eve. Her mother couldn't care less about the time or place of her newest fit of destruction.

Olivia's father pleaded with his wife as he had done so many times before, "Renee, can we just enjoy the holiday without fighting? Please, for Olivia…"

"Haven't I done enough for Olivia? I gave up my life for her! My body, my career, my happiness!"

Olivia could take their incessant bickering no more. Her feet touched the floor beside her bed before she even knew she was leaving. Throwing the door of her bedroom open, she hurriedly marched toward the back of the house.

Without a look back at her parents, Olivia grabbed her coat from the hook, stepped into her boots, and slipped out the back door. No shouting followed her as she crossed the snow-covered yard. Her parents must not have heard her departure over their argument. Even through her coat and jeans, Olivia could feel the chill of the winter evening creeping up her legs and arms.

Being a small town, Joliet only had one grocery store, elementary school, and high school. She had gone to class with the same students since kindergarten, stuck in the revolving cycle of drama and cliques each year. And her mom was right about one thing: everyone knew each other's business.

When she was thirteen, Olivia's dad had taken her shopping in the nearby city. Her mom hated the urban life, claiming skyscrapers and concrete made her feel confined.

She had refused to go. But Olivia and her father loved it – or they loved how far they were from her oppressive mother.

There was a certain liveliness about the city. Whereas Joliet seemed asleep at night, the city was awake every hour of the day. While there were fewer pedestrians and cars later in the evening, neon lights and signs demanded your attention.

As Olivia continued her silent trek, nothing grabbed her attention as she walked down the snow-covered alley toward her grandmother's church. Olivia knew she would find her grandma there at the Christmas Eve service. Vi attended every service at one of Joliet's few churches, rain or shine.

Olivia's chest tightened as she neared the entrance of the church. She knew her mother would disapprove of her stepping foot on any holy ground, especially the very same church that turned its back on her years ago.

But she didn't care what her mom wanted. All Olivia wanted were parents who loved one another and didn't fight every single day of her life. She would even take half-hearted tolerance at this point.

The corridors of the church were vacant of people, the doors to the sanctuary closed. Olivia's body welcomed the warmth of the indoors. The walk in the frigid cold was enough to send chills down her spine.

Slowly and quietly, Olivia crossed the lobby toward the entrance of the chapel, cracking it open and peeking inside. She spotted her grandma near the middle of the room at the end of the pew.

The room was dark except for the soft, warm light provided by a candle in each person's hand. Her grandmother's mouth moved along with the words of the hymn filling the small auditorium.

Olivia hurriedly strode up the aisle and tapped her grandmother's shoulder. Vi looked up in surprise at her granddaughter, checking her from head to toe before smiling in welcome.

She stepped aside to allow room for Olivia, gesturing for her to shed her coat. Once they were settled in the pew, Vi wrapped her arm around her granddaughter and handed her the small white candle. It had a paper disk near the bottom to protect from dripping wax.

This was the first time Olivia had been in a church. She had seen plenty of them on television but had never entered one in fear of repercussions from her mother. If there was one thing her mother didn't need, it was ammunition for her next rant.

The hymn ended and the entire congregation seated themselves, blowing out their candles and turning their attention to the man on a brightly lit stage at the front of the room.

He was a tall, slender man with hair the color of flax. There was a certain charisma, a way about him that demanded your attention. He embodied compassion, kindness, and humor in a way Olivia had never before witnessed.

As she sat listening to his sermon, Olivia noticed several eyes darting in her direction, many of them older women who appeared as if they would drown if it rained too hard.

Yet, as Olivia observed her surroundings while also being careful not to spill hot wax on herself from the candle still in her hands, she noticed a boy around her age near the front of the room looking in her direction.

His hair and eyes appeared dark, the dimmed lights of the room softly illuminating both their warmth and friendliness. Olivia's cheeks turned hot as he continued to observe her for a moment despite her having discovered him, his eyes eventually gravitating back to the pastor.

It was uncommon in a small town like Joliet to see someone new but then again, Olivia remembered her grandmother mentioning the new pastor and his family. That must be his son.

Turning her attention back to the pastor, his words finally resonated in her mind.

"Now, I know we are all tempted this time of year to get overwhelmed by gifts, food, and events. But we need to remember that we don't celebrate earthly possessions we will someday leave behind; we celebrate Christ coming down to Earth to save us from our sins.

He came as an innocent, vulnerable infant… born in a barn, no less. Can you imagine the love He has for us? To leave the glories of Heaven to be born in a manger with filthy barnyard animals?

And that is the most beautiful reason for this joyful season: love. Each and every one of us are recipients of

His love. No matter what you have done, where you have been, or how worthless others have made you feel, you have the unconditional, sacrificial love of Christ. There is no better way to end my sermon than with this message: you... are... loved. Recklessly, stubbornly, and completely loved."

The church stood and sang one final song before the lights illuminated the entire room. Church members grabbed their coats and hugged their friends in farewell, some exchanging gifts wrapped in shiny paper.

Vi stood from the pew and looked down at Olivia who silently remained seated, the words of the sermon repeating in her mind. Something had ignited in her for the first time in her life. She didn't know what it was but her curiosity prevented her from burying it fully in the back of her mind.

"I'm going to assume your mother doesn't know you are at church with me?"

Olivia noticed the stern look on her grandmother's face and hung her head, shrugging off the answer they both knew. When she looked up at her grandmother, prepared for reprimand, Vi had a hint of a smile on her lips.

"Well, I guess it doesn't hurt for us to take our time then, does it? I want to introduce you to some of my friends here."

Olivia met several of her grandmother's friends, mostly older ladies like herself. They all cooed over the granddaughter they had heard so much about, nearly pinching the cheeks of the hesitant teenager.

Finally, they reached the front of the room near the stage when her grandmother came to a stop next to the pastor.

"Wonderful sermon, Pastor. I want you to meet my granddaughter, Olivia. Olivia, this is the new pastor I was telling you about. Pastor Liam James."

The tall, handsome man offered his hand in greeting, a warm smile lighting up his deep blue eyes. In the corners of his eyes were crinkles brought on by years of smiling. His hand swallowed Olivia's during their friendly exchange.

As he took a step back, he placed his hand on the shoulder of a woman with light brown hair and a petite frame. He must have stood at least a foot taller than her, his hand covering the majority of her shoulder.

"This is my wife, Diana. Diana, this is Vi's granddaughter, Olivia."

Diana turned to greet them; her small hand extended as her bright green eyes memorized their faces.

Her voice was warm and sincere when she spoke, "Vi, you told me she was beautiful but I am still blown away. It's nice to finally meet you, Olivia. You are all your grandmother has talked about since we met her some weeks back."

Olivia nodded politely at the pastor and his wife, glancing back at Vi's glowing smile, "It's nice to meet you as well."

"And this is our son, Greyson. Grey, this is Olivia Larson, Vi's granddaughter."

Olivia turned her attention to the boy she had noticed staring at her earlier. In better light, he was much more handsome than she had originally thought.

Both his hair and eyes were lighter than the dim room had allowed her to see. His hair wasn't nearly black but a warm chocolate brown. Yet, it was the color of his eyes that caught her off guard. Instead of dark brown as she had anticipated, they were a warm golden brown, melting into her as he studied her features in turn.

Oh, Grey. I miss you so much.

"It's nice to meet you, Olivia."

She nodded in reply, noticing her grandmother's sly smile as she watched the two interact. Her sharp brown eyes twinkled as she winked at the pastor and his wife who chuckled at the elder woman's suggestive gesture.

"I'll be starting at your school in January as a sophomore."

Olivia noticed that Grey's voice was smooth and deep as he continued their conversation despite the adults stepping away from the group.

"I'm a sophomore, too."

"Oh, so then I'll probably see you in some of our classes. Cool."

She couldn't help but chuckle at Grey's naivety about the tiny town of Joliet. He looked confused by her reaction, uncertain whether her intentions were friendly.

"Joliet is a small town. You will see me all the time. I think we have more cows than we do high school students."

"Oh, well then… even better. Maybe you can show me around… school, not the cows."

Grey looked down at his shuffling feet and laughed, teenage awkwardness in full swing. By the way the other girls their age were ogling him in the corner, he would have no trouble getting shown around campus. Just then, her grandmother tapped her shoulder and looked at her thin gold watch.

"Sorry to interrupt, sugar, but I think it's time we get you home."

"Yeah, I guess so. It was nice to meet you, Greyson. I'll see you at school."

As he returned the farewell, Olivia joined her grandmother and began walking toward the exit.

Even as the girls in the corner called over to him, Grey stood his ground and watched Olivia from across the room. His mother walked up beside him, already shorter than her teenage son.

"Did you like Vi's granddaughter, honey?"

Grey smiled as Olivia disappeared into the foyer, his eyes snapping back to his mother with a wide grin.

"Very much."

Chapter Four

"Do you have any idea how long we looked for you, Olivia? No, you don't because you weren't thinking! We wasted all that time driving around in the snow searching for you."

Olivia's mother was locked and loaded when her grandmother brought her back home.

Her father's voice was much calmer than her mother's but she could see the worry and stress he had endured in losing her, "We were worried about you, Liv. Why did you run away?"

Olivia nearly burned a hole in both of her parents as she glared from the dining table in their direction, "Why do you think I ran away? You guys can't stop fighting… even on Christmas Eve."

"While we are sorry about that, it is no excuse to run away, Olivia. Go to your room. You are grounded for a week."

Ellis looked at his daughter with a seriousness she knew not to challenge. Her mother was still pacing the kitchen, sporadically glowering toward Vi every other step.

"Fine. I don't want to be with either of you anyway. Bye, Grandma. Thanks for the ride. I'll see you Sunday."

Olivia's mother spun on her heel and wiggled her finger from side to side, the opposite hand on her hip, her signature move.

"No, ma'am. You are not going to your grandmother's anymore."

"No, Mom. That's not fair! It's not her fault!"

"I strictly told you never to enter that church. If not for your grandmother shoving religion down your throat, you wouldn't have gone there tonight."

If not for her, I'd be going straight to hell. It's not like you were concerned about me burning for eternity.

"I only went there to be with her. She's the only person who isn't constantly fighting and making me feel worthless!"

"Renee…"

As Olivia's father attempted to protest his wife's punishment, she raised a hand to stop him without taking her scrutinizing eye from Olivia. He shut his mouth and hung his head, closing his eyes in dread.

"Maybe you should get some thicker skin if you don't like to hear the truth. I'm in charge and if I say you don't go to your grandmother's, then you don't! Go to your room *now*!"

Vi's sharp eyes followed Renee's angry movements before they fell on her granddaughter, her shoulders dropping as she caught sight of the broken, young teenager. As she attempted to comfort her granddaughter, she grimaced as if the words tasted bitter.

"It's okay, baby girl. Listen to your mother. I love you."

Renee's expression showed no compassion, her foot tapping impatiently on the floor. Olivia stood from the dining table and ran to the door, throwing her arms around her grandmother with tears in her eyes. Vi was shorter than her but somehow it still felt like she held Olivia up.

"I know, sugar. It's going to be okay. I promise. I love you. You remember that. Nothing will ever change that."

"Olivia, I said go to your room. And, Vi, I want you out of my house."

Vi squeezed her granddaughter around the shoulders before pulling away and placing her hand on the doorknob. Her eyes were misty as she glanced back at her son with a strong air of disappointment. Then, she gave Olivia one last look of sorrow. Renee was the only one not acknowledged during the silent goodbye.

What are you doing, Dad? Say something! It's bad enough I had to live through this in the first place. You just stood there letting your wife call all the shots! You knew she was horrible but you did nothing!

As her grandmother stepped out into the snowy Christmas Eve night, all hope left the house. Olivia ran to her room before the fighting could begin again, throwing herself down on her bed and sobbing into her pillow.

Olivia watched as her younger self wept while curled into a ball on top of her comforter. Yet, something caught her eye she had not noticed that night. Outside the window, Vi could be seen sitting in her car, crying into her hands.

Her soft graying hair bobbed as her shoulders shook with sobs. Out of her childhood bedroom window, Olivia could see her grandmother's mouth moving. Suddenly, she could hear Vi's voice over the sound of her younger self weeping behind her.

"God, please help my girl. Save her from this home, Lord. I don't know what to do anymore. I've prayed and prayed for Renee and Ellis but nothing is changing. Show me what to do, God."

God, I can't listen anymore. Take me away from this house. I don't want to listen to the hours of fighting still to come. I couldn't escape it then but let me leave now.

The furniture in Olivia's room began fading before the rest of the room and the sound of bickering down the hall soon quieted. She was once again in darkness, the purgatory between broken memories.

Please, God, I don't understand why you're making me relive these moments. Wasn't once enough?

Olivia yelled into the darkness to no avail. There was no answer. Instead, yet another memory began to fill her surroundings, allowing no time to protest.

It was the first Sunday morning after being grounded, the sun outside thawing leftover snow from the holiday. Olivia told her mother that she was hanging out with friends and left the house. The desire to see her grandmother motivated her to trudge through the cold mud.

As she walked up the aisle of the church to where her grandmother sat waiting for service to begin, the eyes of several older women scanned her oversized coat, jeans, and mud-covered boots. Her cheeks were red from the cold, hiding the blush creeping up her neck from their scrutiny.

"Olivia, what are you doing here?"

The look on Vi's face evidenced both shock and happiness as she stood from the pew and grabbed her granddaughter in a tight embrace.

"I wanted to see you. Mom doesn't know I'm here."

"Olivia Larson, you're going to bring hellfire down on both of us. Let's get you home right now."

"No, Grandma, please. I don't want to go home. Dad's working and Mom's the only one there. Please, don't make me go home."

Vi's eyes were misty as she pulled Olivia down next to her in the pew, an inner battle displayed in her eyes.

"Okay, sugar. You can stay here with me."

"Please don't tell her I came here. She was so mad last time. You don't have to drive me home. I'll walk… just in case she sees you."

Her mother's angry shouting filled her ears even as she sat surrounded by the murmurs of others' conversations.

"No, I won't have you walking home in this weather."

"Grandma, if she sees you…"

"I'll drop you off a block away from your house. She won't find out. I promise you."

"Thank you, Grandma."

Tears formed in Olivia's eyes as she wrapped her arms around her grandmother, the only person with whom she could truly be vulnerable.

And she never told anyone our secret. Every Sunday, she would pick me up and drop me off a block away from my house, my mom none the wiser.

Music began as the two settled in their seats. Olivia shed her coat and looked around at the other audience members. Once again, she noticed Greyson eyeing her from across the room. But now he had several girls sitting around him, squirming excitedly over their new seating arrangement. Any new cute boy in this town was like a piece of meat circled by vultures.

When the music came to an end and the pastor ascended the small stage, Greyson turned his focus to his father's sermon. Throughout the service, Olivia couldn't help but notice Grey's occasional glance in her direction.

Even Olivia's grandmother noticed his attention, a corner of her mouth lifting in amusement. She nudged Olivia and chuckled under her breath, her reading glasses low on her nose as she flipped through the pages of her Bible.

Olivia dismissed her grandmother's teasing and returned her attention to the pastor.

"…because Christ didn't come to die for perfect people; He died for the murderer, the prostitutes, the hypocrites. That last word should sound familiar to many of us. It's the excuse many people use for not wanting to come to church… the Christians who look down on sinners while they are filthy with their own wrongdoings."

Pastor Liam James was pacing the stage, his hand gestures and moist forehead proof of the level of passion he felt for the subject.

"Church, are you listening to me? Because I want what I say next to be heard with open hearts. We are all sinners deserving the same damnation to hell. Whether you wear your Sunday best every week or sit on the street corner with a cardboard sign in your hands."

Olivia noticed that several of the older women seemed perturbed by his last statement, their noses high enough to sniff out the nearest mouse in the rafters.

"We need to listen to the cries of those outside of this church. Christ did not die for church politics or holier-than-thou attitudes. He died for every single person who has existed and has yet to exist. Who are we to keep that to ourselves?"

Vi rocked in her seat, raising her hand in support of the pastor's words and ignoring dirty looks from several women.

His message echoed in Olivia's ears even as she lay in her bed that night. Her mother hadn't interrogated her when she returned home. There was a glass of wine in her hand as she sat watching television. Her father was out in the garage as usual.

Olivia looked up at the ceiling above her bed, grateful for school starting in the morning. The less time spent at home, the better. As her eyes grew heavy, she replayed the words of Pastor James in her head, a welcome reprieve from her mother's endless criticisms.

Chapter Five

"Have you met Greyson James yet?"

Olivia closed her locker and looked at her best friend, Morgan. Her curly, bright red hair was loose down her back. Her big brown eyes accentuated her round face and the freckles on her nose added a deceptive innocence. She moved to town two years ago and they had been inseparable since.

"Yes, I have. Just like every other girl in the school. Or did you forget that we live in a small town?"

Morgan rolled her eyes at Olivia's sarcastic tone, pushing off from where she stood leaning against the lockers.

"Thank you, Miss Snark. Are you going to tell me exactly how you already met him before his first day at school? A romantic run-in at the grocery store? Were you both reaching for the same juice boxes when your hands touched for the first time?"

Olivia began walking toward her first class of the day, not bothering to check if Morgan and her shorter legs were keeping up with her quick pace.

"You're ridiculous, Morgan. You know that, right?"

Even with an attempted brush-off, Morgan hadn't forgotten her original inquiry as she stared expectantly at her best friend.

"Fine, but you can't tell your parents. Your dad might say something about it to my dad at work."

Morgan's curious eyes widened as she came closer to the answer she sought, "I promise, I promise. Ooh, it must be juicy if you're afraid your parents will find out."

"Yeah, the gossip of the school year. My reputation is ruined entirely at this point."

"You're prettier without the sarcasm, Liv. Now spill."

Olivia chuckled at her best friend's impatience, "We met at my grandma's church. His dad is the new pastor there."

Morgan's face fell in disappointment as Olivia neared her classroom, "Oh, and here I was thinking it was going to be a steamy story. Regardless, you're playing with fire, Liv. You know your mom hates that church."

"Yeah, I know. That's exactly why I asked you to keep it a secret. It's one of the only ways I can see my grandma. She and mom aren't necessarily getting along right now."

"Fine. I'll keep your secret… but only if you admit that Greyson James is a beautiful specimen."

Olivia looked up at the clock in the hallway, realizing there were only a couple of minutes left until the tardy bell, "No. You know I'm not interested in any boy. Save your breath."

"Oh, come on. I'm not leaving until you say it. You'll be the reason I'm late to class."

"Ugh. Whatever. Yes, he's cute."

Morgan put her hand behind her ear as if she were struggling to hear her friend not three feet away, "I don't think I heard you correctly. Who do you think is cute?"

Olivia knew this would never end if she didn't do exactly what her friend was asking of her. She grabbed Morgan and spun her around in the direction of her class, "Greyson James is a beautiful specimen. There! Are you happy?"

As soon as Olivia turned around toward her classroom, she regretted ever saying his name. There Greyson sat in the second row, looking directly at her with a sly grin on his face.

She heard Morgan's laughter from the hallway, knowing fully that her best friend intentionally set her up. Not only did she earn the attention of Greyson James but of several girls surrounding him.

It didn't matter that he had four different girls standing around his desk, Greyson's caramel brown eyes followed Olivia as she took the only empty desk two seats behind him.

She could feel the heat of his stare creep up her neck as she organized her books on her desk and kept her head down.

"Hey, man. Do you mind if we switch desks?"

Olivia looked up from her books quickly to find the laid-back skater in front of her giving up his seat to Greyson. Before she could protest, Grey sat down and turned around to face her, the golden-brown of his eyes twinkling.

"I was hoping we would share a class or two."

Olivia kept her focus on her pencil, tapping it against the spine of her notebook. He seemed entertained by her nonchalant attitude.

"Yeah, small town, remember?"

Grey paused for a moment as several girls purposefully walked through the aisle where his long legs were stretched. He politely moved his legs but failed to give them the attention they sought. Instead, he kept his eyes on Olivia.

"Who was your friend in the hallway? I'm not sure I have met her yet."

"Morgan Hughes. What? You don't have enough options already with the half dozen girls staring at you in this class alone?"

If Greyson was surprised by her cynicism, he hid it well, "I was merely curious about who you were friends with. But now that we're on the subject… what is with the girls in this town? It's like I'm the last boy on earth."

"You're fresh meat. The vultures always swarm around the newest victim. It will wear off eventually so enjoy it while you can."

"What makes you think I enjoy it?"

He lifted his dark brows inquisitively, waiting patiently for Olivia to respond.

"Don't all guys think the same way? You've got your choice of every girl in town and you're wasting your time talking to me. Better go play the field."

Grey chuckled under his breath, rubbing his hand on the back of his neck where his hair lay, "You think you have all men figured out, huh?"

Before Olivia could answer his question, the teacher began class. Grey's eyes scanned her face one last time before he hesitantly turned around in his seat.

Whatever his motive was in talking to her and staring at her in church, she refused to fall for any guy in high school. Her mother had gotten pregnant from a high school romance and she refused to follow in her footsteps.

If Olivia knew one thing, it was that she didn't want to be anything like her mom, bitter and angry from the way her life turned out.

Though she tried as hard as she could, Olivia could not keep her eyes from the back of Greyson's head during class: the minuscule golden highlights running through the chocolate brown of his hair and the freckle on the right side of his neck.

Before she knew it, the bell rang for the next class period. Olivia grabbed her books and whisked past Greyson before he had a chance to turn around again. Whatever his game was, she refused to be a pawn in it.

"So, where can you go around here for a good burger and milkshake?"

That boy held my heart long before I admitted it.

Olivia glanced in the direction of the voice, Grey effortlessly matching her brisk pace.

"The café on the corner of Main and Brookside, Sandy's. Best burgers in town."

"Awesome. I've been craving one since we moved here. You want to go with me on Saturday?"

Her feet came to a halt in the middle of the hallway, forcing several students to veer around them. Grey furrowed his brow in confusion, spinning on his heel to face her.

"Thank you for the offer, Greyson, but I can't."

"Can't or won't?"

Olivia let out a sigh, her patience waning, "Why does it matter? The answer is still the same."

"Look, I don't know what I did to offend you but I'm sorry. I just thought we could grab a burger together."

"Yeah, it will start with a burger... which leads to dating which leads to kissing, then sex, and then a baby. And that's not a path I'm going down. So, have your pick of the countless girls chasing you, but I'm not one of them."

Grey's curious expression turned into one of shock as Olivia pushed past him and continued to her next class. She felt guilt over her outburst but knew it needed to be done. He wasn't the first boy she had rejected for the same reason, nor would he be the last.

At the end of the school day, Olivia opened her locker to grab her belongings before heading home. As she pulled the metal door open, she noticed a small note shoved through the vent.

Olivia glanced around the bustling hallway for who might have left the note but found no suspicious characters. She unfolded it from its triangular shape, finding a drawing of a burger with an animated expression.

It had large, round eyes and a smile wider than the hamburger bun. Next to it was a dialogue bubble that read, "The offer still stands. Just burgers."

Much to her chagrin, Olivia found herself smiling, not just at the silly drawing, but at the offer. There was something genuinely honest about Grey that made her believe him.

As she took her seat behind Greyson the next morning, she tapped his shoulder. He turned around, his eyebrows raised in question.

She smiled hesitantly as she offered him a small triangle of paper just as the teacher was starting the lecture.

Grey turned toward the front of the class and opened the note discretely.

Next to the drawing of the hamburger was a milkshake, its gloved hand waving off the page. It too had a bubble next to it which read, "What about the milkshakes?"

Olivia smiled when she heard a soft chuckle come from Grey as he shoved the note into his pocket. Ever so slightly, he nodded his head in confirmation while keeping his attention on the whiteboard.

Though there was a pit in her stomach warning against the decision to hang out with Greyson, something in the back of her mind stopped her from overthinking it.

After all, it was just burgers… and milkshakes.

Chapter Six

"You weren't kidding when you said how good these burgers are. Oh, man!"

Across the table, Greyson seemed to be genuinely enjoying the burger, juices running down his hands as he took another large bite. There was something unnatural about how much teenage boys could eat in one sitting.

"I wouldn't joke about something as important as a good burger. It's one of my main food groups. That and chocolate."

"Hopefully not together. That would be quite a mixture."

Grey's husky chuckle was infectious as the two sat in the small diner eating burgers on Saturday afternoon.

Several of their classmates from school were there, too, eyeing them curiously from across the room.

Yet again, Greyson seemed unaffected by the attention he received from so many girls. He focused only on Olivia and the juicy burger in his hands.

Olivia smiled, studying the thick beef patty sandwiched between two pillowy buns and melted cheese before taking a bite, "No, not together. But I can't say I haven't tried."

"Please tell me you're joking. How'd you do it? Chocolate syrup instead of ketchup?"

Grey's eyes twinkled with humor as he waited for Olivia's response. She took a sip of her milkshake before shrugging, "You know how they put squares of chocolate in a smores?"

"You didn't."

"Yup. That's exactly what I did. It melted just like it would on a smores. Let's just say I prefer my chocolate beefless."

Grey made a face of disgust at her statement as he pushed his now empty plate away from him, pulling his milkshake to his mouth.

Olivia studied him as he looked around at the eclectic decorations on the café walls. He seemed confident in himself without being arrogant, relaxed even when given attention, and all-around likable.

During the past week of school, they had talked before and after first period. Much to the disappointment of the desperate girls in class, Grey remained absorbed in his conversations with Olivia, earning her countless glares in the hallway.

Between classes, she would find notes shoved in her locker, each with a humorous drawing or joke. Although Olivia wasn't interested in dating during high school, she couldn't help but be drawn to Grey, even if just for friendship.

"So, where did you live before moving here?"

Grey took his caramel eyes from the vintage soda pop sign above their table and returned his attention to Olivia, "Jasper, Pennsylvania. It is a suburb close to the city, probably three or four times the size of Joliet."

"Must have been a shock moving here then. Why would your family choose this town anyway?"

"My dad wanted to move to a smaller town, get away from the city. He interviewed with the church here and got an offer the next day. Why? What's so bad about this town?"

"It's too small. Everyone knows your business. I want to be more than this tiny town allows. I just want to get away, you know?"

Grey studied her as she took a sip of her milkshake and leaned back in the booth they occupied. He mulled over her answer before appearing to change the subject intentionally.

"Will I see you at church tomorrow?"

"Yeah, I should be able to make it."

He tilted his head to the side inquisitively, "*Should* be?"

Olivia looked down at her hands in her lap and took a deep breath before meeting eye contact with Grey again, "Long story."

Grey looked pointedly at the clock on the wall and propped his elbows on the table, his caramel brown eyes focused on hers. He eagerly awaited her explanation. After a moment of hesitation, Olivia sighed.

There was no harm in telling him about her mom. Plus, Grey had a comforting and trustworthy presence which made her believe he would keep her secret.

"My mom doesn't want me going to church… or seeing my grandma. She thinks I am hanging out with friends every Sunday."

Grey seemed caught off guard by her situation, clearly not expecting such a formidable excuse. He shifted in his seat before clearing his throat, a soft tone escaping his lips when he spoke, "Why doesn't she want you going to church?"

"She went there before getting pregnant with me as a teenager. They kicked her and my dad out and refused to marry them. Ever since then, she has hated church entirely."

Hated everything actually.

"Wow. That's terrible. I can't believe they did that."

Olivia raised a single eyebrow in question, "Is that really so unbelievable?"

He straightened his posture and searched the table as if the answer lay there, "What do you mean?"

"Don't you see how people look at me when I walk into the church? I've never felt more judged in my entire life. It makes me understand a small part of what my mother went through."

"I'm so sorry. I never noticed anyone else looking at you… What about your dad? How does he feel?"

"My dad is not nearly as bitter about his past as my mother. She's let it consume her entirely. Bitterness is like cancer; it spreads until everything is dead. My mom's humanity died the moment she found out I existed."

Grey furrowed his brow and stretched his arm across the table where Olivia now fidgeted with her napkin. His large hand was warm as it enveloped hers, electricity coursing through her arm from his touch.

"Don't say that, Liv. I'm sure she loves you. God has a plan and a purpose for everything. Maybe if you just invite her to come tomorrow…"

Olivia interrupted him before he could finish his sentence, "No. I knew it was a mistake talking about this. I don't need you to get all churchy and make my home life even worse. Just forget about it."

She went to grab her coat from beside her when Grey leaned over the table, his hand resting gently on her shoulder and his warm eyes melting into hers, "Hey, hey. I didn't mean to upset you. I'm sorry. Please stay."

Olivia looked around the room to check for an audience before releasing the soft cotton of her coat. Grey seemed relieved when she settled back into her seat.

"So, tell me, Olivia Larson, what do you want to do when you move to the big city?"

His ability to affect her mood so easily both terrified and calmed her. There was no denying Grey's attitude was infectious to every person with whom he spoke but there was a connection to Olivia that trumped all others.

It was this connection that magnetized them to one another. They talked about their aspirations, fears, embarrassing childhood stories, and favorite foods.

When it was finally time to part, Grey stood outside his parents' car, his father waiting patiently in the driver's seat.

"Can I offer you a ride home?"

Olivia shuffled her feet, trying to stay warm in the below-freezing temperatures outside, "No, I'm fine. I like to walk."

"It's really no problem. It's so cold and I would feel terrible if you had to walk all the way home."

"My mom would kill me if she found out I was with a boy this whole time. She's afraid I'll repeat her past and end up pregnant in high school, too."

"Okay. I don't want to make her mad. Well, I'll see you tomorrow then… hopefully. I enjoyed hanging out with you."

His eyes twinkled as he looked down at her before climbing into the passenger seat of his car. Olivia returned his father's wave as they drove away from the café.

When she returned home, Olivia found her father waiting for her at the kitchen table. He looked exhausted, his eyes red from tears shed and his hair tussled from anxious hands.

"Olivia, we need to talk."

No, God, stop. Please, I'm begging you. Don't make me watch anymore. I can't go through this. Not again. Please.

Yet, God had a different plan for her. The memories continued as Olivia relived one of the worst parts of her life.

Chapter Seven

Though Olivia attempted to stop the memory from replaying, there was nothing she could do as her fifteen-year-old self sat down at the dining table with her father.

Please, God, no. I can't do it again.

"Olivia, I need to tell you… this isn't easy to say."

His voice cracked as he looked down at his worn hands on the table, something Olivia rarely saw from her father. After countless fights with her mother, he had learned to shut off his emotions.

"Dad, if you're going to tell me that you and mom are getting a divorce, I already know. I heard you talking about it last week."

Ellis leaned forward in his chair, his eyes wide in shock from her confession. But his expression showed there was more to the conversation than their divorce.

"Yes, we are getting divorced, Olivia. And we'll talk about that later but right now, there is something else you need to know."

Olivia questioned what could possibly be bigger news in her life than her parents divorcing. She watched as her father's eyes welled up with tears.

"Your grandmother passed away this morning. I'm so sorry, Liv."

At first, Olivia could find no words. It couldn't be true. Her grandmother was perfectly healthy and as much of a spitfire as ever.

"What? How?"

Olivia managed to spit out single-word questions as the heaviness in her chest continued to expand.

"When she didn't show up for her prayer meeting at the church, a few of her friends became concerned. She had given them my number as her emergency contact. I went right over to her house after they called and she… just never woke up."

The weight of reality crashed down on Olivia like a wave in the ocean, pushing her down then pulling her deeper. Her vision became blurred as tears burned in her eyes.

Her father's arms wrapped around her just as her world began to crumble to a million pieces, a world without her grandma.

***

The funeral for her grandmother was held at the church. Her casket sat in front of the pulpit surrounded by several arrangements of white flowers.

With the divorce underway, her father ignored his wife's hatred for the church and held the service there as his mother had wanted. After weeks of attending church, Olivia thought it felt odd sitting in the pew without her grandmother next to her. Instead, her dad sat beside her in his dark suit, bags under his eyes from the loss of his mother.

Olivia wasn't surprised that her mother refused to attend the service based on the contempt she held for both her mother-in-law and the church. If she had to admit it to herself, Olivia was glad her mother wasn't there. The last thing she needed was to endure another bitter comment at the expense of her beloved grandma.

Even as her daughter and husband of fifteen years mourned for Vi, Renee refused to break from tradition, continuing with her sour attitude and rude remarks.

Grey's father spoke during the service on the subject of heaven and the promise God had given His followers of a glorious paradise. He spoke of Vi's sassy and blunt personality, citing several occasions where she spoke honestly at church events.

Ellis chuckled under his breath at the reputation his mother had left behind, tears filling the corners of his eyes as he glanced down at his hands in his lap.

Olivia watched as he collected himself and returned his gaze to the pastor at the front of the room. Ellis noticed the attention he was receiving from his daughter and wrapped his arm around her shoulders. He pulled her into his side and squeezed tight, placing a tender kiss on top of her head.

She melted under his arm, desperate for some kind of comfort in the ocean of grief in which she was drowning. When it was time to stand next to the casket and accept condolences from the guests, Olivia placed herself beside her father with her grandmother on his opposite side.

If she stood next to Vi, she knew her emotions would get the best of her. She held her composure as both familiar and unfamiliar faces greeted her.

At the end of the line, Grey and his parents introduced themselves to her father and shared kind words about Vi. Diana James stepped toward Olivia with a tender smile on her face, her green eyes glistening with emotion.

"How are you doing, my dear?"

Her hands were warm on Olivia's arms as she studied her face. Olivia fought the urge to break down, shrugging her shoulders.

"As good as I can be, I guess. I'm really going to miss her."

"We all will, Olivia. She was just that good of a person. But she will never truly die, not when there are so many people who she has impacted positively. She will live on through us, dear. Through you."

I wish I had a mom like her.

Olivia's eyes began to water as she dropped her head and nodded, feeling one last squeeze from Diana before she released her and walked away.

Where there were once high heels in front of her own feet now stood dark men's shoes. When she looked up, Olivia found warm caramel eyes, once twinkling with humor but now filled with sorrow. Dark lashes shadowed the gold of his eyes. Greyson.

She didn't know what it was about him that compelled her to step toward Greyson and wrap her arms around his waist; she just knew she was exhausted from holding herself together all day.

At first, Grey tensed in surprise at Olivia's sudden and unexpected behavior but relaxed as she buried her face in his shirt. Deep sobs reverberated through her body as he placed his arms around her, one hand on her back and one cradling the nape of her neck.

Grey's father, still speaking with Ellis, turned to look at the spectacle, both surprise and empathy filling his expression. All eyes were on Olivia and Grey as they remained locked in their embrace, too absorbed in one another to notice the attention they received.

Liam stepped toward his son and whispered in his ear before returning to his conversation with Olivia's father, gesturing toward the two adolescents. Ellis glanced at his daughter in concern before nodding in approval to Grey.

With one single nod, Grey bent down to murmur in Olivia's ear, "Olivia, I'm going to take you out of the sanctuary. Your dad said it's okay."

Still overcome with sobbing, Olivia allowed Grey to guide her out of the auditorium and into one of the Sunday school classrooms in the hallway toward the back of the church.

She heard the door shut behind them before Grey seated her on a cold metal chair and wrapped his coat around her shoulders. He pulled a chair beside her and drew her against him, laying her head on his chest as she struggled to catch her breath from weeping.

"Shhh. It's okay, Liv. Just let it out."

Grey rubbed his thumb against her shoulder and laid his cheek against the top of Olivia's head, holding her steady as another wave of sobs shook her.

Make the memories stop here, God. Just let me stay in his arms.

The two sat alone in the small classroom with only the sound of Olivia's crying filling the silence. When there were no more tears to cry, Grey grabbed tissues from the small wooden coffee table in the center of the room.

He offered them to Olivia, patiently waiting as she dried her face and wiped away the remnants of her makeup. When she looked up at him with red eyes, he smiled tenderly and pushed a strand of hair from her face.

"I'm sorry, Greyson. I didn't mean to break down like that. I shouldn't have…"

"Don't apologize. I'm glad I could be there for you."

Olivia skimmed her eyes over Grey, noticing the black button-up shirt and charcoal gray slacks he wore. She couldn't help but think how handsome he looked in the outfit.

A dark spot where Olivia had rested her head could be seen on his shirt.

"I'm sorry for getting your shirt wet."

"I won't melt. I promise."

His smile reached his eyes now as his face lit up with humor. The warmth and comfort of his personality drew Olivia in and tore down walls she had placed around herself from living with constant battering from her mother.

"My life is such a mess right now. My parents are getting a divorce and the one person I could talk to about everything is gone forever."

"I know I could never replace Vi but I want you to know that you can always talk to me, Olivia."

"Thanks, Grey, for everything. I should get back to my dad now."

"Yeah, probably. I'm glad you're okay, Olivia. When you didn't come to church Sunday, I thought something had happened with your mom or maybe you just didn't want to see me. Then, I heard about Vi…"

"I… I couldn't sit in that pew without her a day after she died."

"Well, you can always sit by me. If you want."

Grey's eyes were vulnerable as he brought his gaze up from his shoes to her face. Olivia stood from the metal chair and shrugged off his coat, handing it back to him before starting for the door. She turned and found him standing, waiting for a response.

"I'm not sure how much I'll come to church without my grandma. She was the reason I came."

"Well, I hope you find another reason. The seat will be saved for you no matter your decision."

As she turned the door knob, Olivia attempted a genuine smile as she prepared to face the world of mourning outside the small room where they had been hidden, "Thank you, Grey."

As the fifteen-year-old returned to the funeral service, the older Olivia stayed behind with Grey. He stood in the same spot, studying the coat in his hands. His fingers grazed the soft material tenderly as he returned his gaze to the now empty doorway.

Then, Grey bowed his head and closed his eyes. It was something Olivia had witnessed her husband do countless times over the years.

He was praying. For me.

Chapter Eight

Olivia dreaded going back to school after her grandmother's funeral. Not only would everyone know about Vi's passing, but would feel the need to apologize for her loss and be overly friendly all day.

And to add to the heap of dread Olivia felt as she walked down the hallway, Grey stood leaning against her locker waiting for her.

"Hey, Olivia. How are you?"

She crossed her arms over her chest and sighed before replying to his question, "Are you going to be weird all day, too? Because I've already received like ten apologies and half a dozen sympathetic faces just walking down this hallway."

Grey pushed himself from her locker as she stepped forward and removed the lock. He remained at a respectful distance behind her as she gathered her books for class.

"Am I being weird? Hmm… I must not know the norms here in Joliet yet. Where I'm from, that's a common greeting."

Olivia spun around to see a smirk across his soft lips, a mischievous look in his warm caramel eyes.

"I just don't want things to be weird after what happened at the funeral."

"Who said it has to be weird? I've had hundreds of people cry on me like that."

She couldn't help but smile as they walked together to their shared first class.

"Hundreds? What is it that makes you the ideal tissue?"

"It's a mixture of compassion, absorbent shirts, and, above all, deodorant. No one wants a human tissue that smells like the boys' locker room after P.E."

"Yeah, I've been meaning to mention that to one of your sex. Cologne does not mask the smell; it just mixes to make an all-new assault to the senses."

"Noted. I will mention it at our next meeting. It's every Wednesday. A guy named Tim brings donuts."

And, in an instant, any resistance toward becoming friends with Grey ceased to exist.

4 MONTHS LATER

"What do you mean you're moving to the city?"

Olivia looked at her father in disbelief as he packed the last of his possessions into the truck one Sunday morning. It had been four months since her grandmother passed. Since the funeral, her mom and dad had been preparing to separate and file for divorce.

Previously, when her parents sat down to talk with their daughter about the transition, it was planned that her father would stay in town at his place, equally sharing custody of Olivia throughout the week and weekend. However, their plans were upended at the last minute with her dad's new job offer.

"I'm sorry, Liv. It all happened so quickly. My boss referred me to the company's headquarters in the city and they offered me the job the next day. I didn't think I even had a chance at getting the position. A floor manager getting a job at corporate?"

"And you didn't think to mention it until you're packing your stuff to leave? What does that mean about where I'm going to live?"

Her dad closed the bed of his truck and wiped his hands on his jeans before stepping toward where Olivia stood in the driveway.

"Your mother and I thought that since you only had a couple of years left of high school, it would make the most sense for you to finish your schooling here."

"So, you're just leaving me with her?"

Olivia gestured sharply toward the house where her mother was either watching them from the window or drinking wine in the living room.

"Liv, it's going to be okay. Your mother and I fight all the time. Without me here, it will get better. Plus, you can still come to see me on weekends and anytime during the summer. It's less than an hour away."

"Dad, please don't leave me with her. She hates me. Honestly, I think she hates everyone. All she does is sit around and drink all day. When she's not doing that, she's criticizing me."

"Maybe she'll be happier when she starts her new job. She'll be working at that insurance office downtown during the week."

Wishful thinking.

"Nothing makes that woman happy. You know I love the city, Dad. Why can't I just live with you? I'll change schools. I'll make new friends and graduate there."

Ellis shook his head and shoved his hands into the pockets of his jeans. Olivia knew that look. There was nothing she could say that would change his mind.

Anger welled up in her throat and her vision started to blur with hot tears. Her feet began to move though she had no idea where she was going.

Olivia could hear her father calling out to her as she ran down their road, rounding a corner before he could get in his truck and follow her. The t-shirt and shorts she wore dampened with perspiration as she turned down another street.

Breathlessly, Olivia stopped in her tracks as she looked up at the familiar steeple of her grandmother's church.

Having left her phone at home after running from her dad, Olivia had no idea what time it was. The church service could have been over for all she knew. But at that moment, she needed to feel close to two different people: her grandmother and Grey.

Even though Greyson promised to save her a seat every Sunday, she doubted he could keep the female vultures away too long. Not to mention, she hadn't attended church since her grandmother passed four months ago.

She hadn't been able to bring herself to walk through the corridors knowing Vi wouldn't be there to greet her with a warm smile and a squeeze of the shoulders.

However much doubt Olivia had felt before, the heartbreak she was feeling urged her forward. She walked through the exterior doors and strode across the foyer to the doors of the sanctuary. The clock on the wall told her that she hadn't missed the service. It had begun only twenty minutes prior to her arrival.

Olivia cracked open the door to let herself through when the sound of squeaky hinges filled the large room. All eyes were on her as she stood in shock at the door's betrayal. Yet, only one pair of eyes at the front of the room caught her attention.

Grey was sitting next to his mother as always, grinning from ear to ear as the room continued to scrutinize her late arrival. Olivia realized she was far too casual for church in her t-shirt and shorts.

Grey's dad stood on the stage, briefly taking in the situation before continuing with his sermon. She was beyond grateful for his distraction as the audience members returned their focus on the pastor.

Olivia walked down the aisle on the side of the room toward Grey and noticed the empty spot beside him. With his long, masculine fingers, he patted the pew next to him in invitation.

As Olivia sat down and adjusted her wind-blown hair, she did her best not to draw any more attention to herself. Grey silently mouthed if she was okay to which she merely nodded her head. He studied her for a moment before returning his focus to his father.

Pastor Liam James wore a dark navy-blue suit with a crisp white shirt. There was no doubt he was a handsome man but as she studied him, Olivia couldn't help but notice the lack of common features between him and his son.

The differences began to pile up. Grey had light caramel brown eyes while his father had deep blue. His father had flaxen blonde hair, sharp features, and thick, wide hands. Grey had chocolate brown hair, a strong jawline, and long, slender fingers.

Olivia made a note to compare Grey to his mother later and gave her full attention to the stage. Pastor James stood at the pulpit, a single Bible laying before him.

"Our God is not a God who fails us; we fail Him. And yet, He will never leave us. He is our heavenly Father. Did you catch that? Our *heavenly* Father. Plenty of us have earthly relationships that have failed us. Maybe you've never met your father or connected with your mother.

No matter the hurt our earthly relationships have caused us, we have a God who sent His Son to die for our sins. All those stupid choices we've made in our lives, all those mistakes that still haunt us.

His love is unconditional, unlimited, and unending. It doesn't matter how much money or success you have, the clothes you wear, or the car you drive. He is a Father who will never stop chasing after your love.

I know it sounds too good to be true. You may be asking yourself why the God of creation might pursue you so recklessly. Those of you who are parents might understand a small part of His love for us.

When I held my son in my arms for the first time, I knew I would go to hell and back for that boy. No matter his choices in life or the mistakes he would make, I would eternally love him with my entire being.

It wasn't until God gave Greyson to my wife and me that I grasped that kind of love. We as humans cannot begin to fathom God's love. When we deserved His full wrath, He sacrificed His only beloved Son to take our place, bearing the suffocating weight of our sins.

Let us rejoice for our Father, the God who created us, who picks us up when we fall, and loves us when we are unlovable. For those of you who are still bleeding from that hole in your heart, fill it with God today. Run into the arms of your Father and never look back. He has changed me and He can change you. Won't you come?"

The band began to play and the lump in Olivia's throat only grew as Pastor James stood in the center aisle waiting for those needing prayer. The pulling Olivia had felt since the first time she stepped through the doors of the church became overwhelming.

Stop fighting it.

She shifted in her chair and rubbed her hands together anxiously in her lap. Tears began to stream down her cheeks when a large warm hand clasped over her nervous fingers.

Grey's warm breath sent chills down her back as he whispered in her ear, "Liv, are you okay? Do you need to talk to someone?"

She nodded her head in confirmation, giving in to the pulling of her heart. He guided her to stand but instead of leading her before the entire church, he merely switched her seats so that she sat next to his mother.

Diana's kind and comforting voice greeted her along with a tender touch of her hand on Olivia's shoulder, "What's wrong, dear?"

"I'm not worth the kind of love your husband talks about."

"Oh, honey, but that's the point. None of us deserve the mercy God gives us. That's what makes Him God. His love is unbelievably beautiful."

Olivia wiped the tears from her eyes with the tissue Diana placed in her hand. She couldn't conceive of God's love when all she heard in her mind were her mother's bitter criticisms reminding her that she wasn't good enough.

"I can tell you're fighting something inside yourself, Olivia. Block everything else out and focus on *you*. What is it that *you* want to do?"

Fighting with all of her might, Olivia pushed the echoes of her mother's words out of her mind, if only for the moment. She swallowed hard against the ache in her chest and nodded her head, "I think I need to pray… but I don't know how."

"Just talk to God, dear. There is no wrong way to pray. Tell Him what is on your mind."

Olivia swallowed hard as she fought to speak the words caught in her throat.

"God, I feel so alone. My life is falling apart and I can't do anything about it. I know You sacrificed Your Son so that my sins could be forgiven. Please come into my life. I can't do this by myself."

As soon as she finished her prayer, the aching of her heart and the magnetic pull of her soul to the church was eased. She felt relief and for a moment, there was no doubt, no despair, and no words from her mother echoing in her mind. There was only hope.

Chapter Nine

"I'm just saying that maybe there's a better burger out there."

Greyson's dark brown wavy hair was unkempt as the wind blew through the windows of his car. His warm caramel eyes were bright as he looked to the passenger seat where Olivia sat with her knees drawn up.

"How dare you say that, Grey! You've eaten Sandy's burgers for over a year and you're just going to stab her in the back like that?"

"There will be no stabbing. All I mean is that it's a big world full of delicious burgers. Maybe there's one we could find that is better than Sandy's."

Olivia continued to feign anger as Grey pulled to the side of the road in front of her house. It was the last day of their junior year and summer break had just begun for the small town of Joliet.

After she accepted his saved seat at church, Grey and Olivia had been attached at the hip. They sat together during school lunches, hung out on weekends, and saved one another seats at church.

When Olivia and Grey first began their friendship, Morgan could not resist countless comments about their relationship and its romantic potential. However, after over a year of a strictly platonic friendship, she was just happy to have another friend in their circle.

The vultures at school calmed their desperate hunting to a mere interest in Greyson. Although he was kind to everyone, there never seemed to be a girl who caught his attention. He was too busy talking to Olivia to notice anyone else.

"Are you coming tomorrow, Grey?"

Olivia looked over at Greyson in the driver's seat with raised eyebrows, her hand resting on the door handle.

"What's tomorrow?"

"I'm meeting Morgan at her house and we're heading down to the lake. A bunch of people from school are getting together. There will be food, games, and swimming. I think there's even one of those ropes you swing into the water."

"Sounds like fun. I'll be there. Can I give you a ride?"

"That'd be great. Thank you. The party starts at one and I said I'd meet Morgan at her house at noon. She takes forever to pick out an outfit."

Grey chuckled at the remark, knowing Morgan's struggle with time all too well by now, "Okay. I'll pick you up a little before noon."

"Awesome. Thanks again. See you then."

"Bye, Liv."

Grey remained in the car as Olivia walked to her front door, waiting until she was safely inside to drive away.

"Was that a boy you were with, Olivia?"

Olivia jumped at the sound of her mother's voice. Her mother must've gotten home from work early and parked her car in the garage. She had been watching Olivia and Grey from the front window the entire time.

"Yeah, that's my friend, Greyson."

"Friend, huh? Are you having sex with him?"

Her mother's face was stern as she prodded at her daughter's personal life, her hand on her hip as usual.

"Mom, no! I said he's just a friend. Please, I can't hear your same lecture for the millionth time. I'm not having sex or dating and I'm not going to get pregnant in high school."

"Yeah, I wish I could believe you."

I wish you could, too.

Olivia rolled her eyes as she walked down the hallway to her bedroom, doing her best to ignore the part of the conversation where her mother picked apart her every action.

Her room had changed subtly from her childhood. The purple comforter had been replaced by an oversized, fluffy tie-dyed duvet. Though the furniture remained the same, the atmosphere had changed drastically.

There were clothes and shoes scattered across the floor and a lack of family photos on the walls and tabletops. Instead of the cute girlish posters of horses on the wall, there were pictures of her favorite bands and celebrities.

After throwing together a change of clothes for tomorrow and finding her swimsuit from last summer, Olivia got ready for bed and laid down.

She heard the television in the next room blaring a soap opera. Olivia could just picture her mother in her usual spot on the couch with a second or third glass of wine in hand.

Her mother's drinking had always been casual, at meals or the end of a long day. But ever since the divorce, the number of glasses increased and the number of empty wine bottles in the trash piled up.

Olivia turned over on her stomach and looked at the picture frame on her bedside table. The photo was of her with Morgan sticking her tongue out and Grey smiling brightly.

It had been taken one Saturday at Sandy's café. She remembered the girls in the corner of the room giggling and gesturing toward Grey, failing to hide their giddiness at his presence.

Yet again, he behaved as if there were no girls in the room. Olivia's eyes landed on his smiling face in the photo as her eyes grew heavy, a question lingering in her mind as she drifted off to sleep.

***

"Do you want to go back to the picnic tables?"

Grey's eyes were soft as he looked down at Olivia. He wore only swim trunks, allowing his smooth chest to be kissed by the afternoon sunlight. Water dripped from his dark brown hair, acquired from his first rope swing into the lake.

Olivia wore her bathing suit, a melon-colored bikini with frayed jean shorts over her bottoms. Her delicate curves filled out her swimsuit and her long dark hair was held high in a messy bun. She remained dry, having chickened out from her jump following Grey.

When his cheering couldn't motivate her to jump, Grey swam out of the lake and ascended the hill once more. At the bottom of the hill next to the beach, their classmates mingled at their end-of-school-year picnic.

Olivia shook her head and gripped the rope tightly, eyeing the shimmering water down below. She could smell Grey's scent from where he stood close by, a masculine mixture of sandalwood and citrus accentuated by the water from the lake.

"No, I can do it. I've just never been a fan of heights, that's all."

"We can go together…"

Grey's expression demonstrated his respect for Olivia and his desire not to cross any lines. As she looked into his honey brown eyes, she felt the same comfort she had since the day of her grandmother's funeral. With him, Olivia knew she was safe.

"Okay. But you can't do what parents do when they're teaching you to ride a bike and let go."

Grey's voice was shaky as he pulled her close and grabbed hold of the rope, "I promise I won't let you go."

Olivia tensed as his arms wrapped around her, the warm scent of him filling her nostrils. She clutched the rope and let him envelop her completely.

"Should I call you Tarzan then?"

Grey's deep chuckle vibrated against her back where his firm chest was pressed, "Only if I can call you Jane."

His breath was warm against her ear as he spoke softly, sending a pleasant chill down her spine. Olivia was very aware of Grey: his smell, his touch, even his breathing.

He was consuming, the comfort she had grown familiar with as a friend now a magnet drawing her desires from deep within. Her thoughts were not those of a friend as she attempted to hide the blush sweeping across her cheeks.

"Are you ready, Liv?"

Olivia licked her lips, her fear of heights being the last thing on her mind, "Um, yeah."

With Grey's guidance, she stepped off the rocky cliff hanging from the side of the hill and gripped the rope with all her might. His body tightened around her as he held onto the rope then loosened as they both fell to the water down below.

The two separated mid-fall, landing away from each other in the water. When she broke the surface, Grey was already swimming toward her.

Olivia's feet failed to touch the bottom of the lake, requiring her to keep herself above the water with robust swings of her arms and legs.

"Are you okay, Liv?"

"Yeah, I'm fine. It wasn't as bad as I thought it would be. Can you reach the bottom?"

Grey stopped swimming when he was a few feet away from her. His caramel eyes seemed lighter in the sunlight as he studied her face.

"No, I can't."

They both swam closer to the shore until they no longer had to fight to stay above the water, their feet hitting the cool mud of the lake floor.

When she turned, Grey was within arm's length still focused on her. Olivia blushed under his intense study. Never before had she seen Grey with such a penetrating expression as he swam even closer to her in the water.

His shaggy brown hair was disheveled, his hands having run through the dripping strands. Olivia was aware of his focus on her lips but couldn't bring herself to break his concentration.

To her surprise, she didn't want him at a distance. She didn't find discomfort in his intensity; she found desire, a desire to be held and a need to taste his lips.

The water rippled over them as they stayed in their trance, studying one another with new eyes. Friendship gave way to something new, something bigger than the both of them.

Grey continued to search her face for any sign of disapproval as his hands found her waist and pulled her against him. His body was firm, the wiry muscles pulling his smooth skin taut against his frame.

The warmth of his body was welcome in the cool water. Olivia's hands found the nape of his neck, strands of his wet hair running between her fingers.

It was then that something in Grey seemed to snap, his lips meeting hers gently at first and then firmer as she pushed her body harder against his.

His passion remained controlled as he pulled away from her. Olivia dropped her hands and studied the golden brown of his eyes alive with adrenaline.

I love the way his eyes look after we've kissed.

The voices of their classmates filled the air once more as they both returned to reality. No one seemed to notice their kiss as they went about their activities of beach volleyball, gossiping, and eating.

Grey looked around for any audience members before hesitantly turning back to Olivia, "Liv, I'm sorry."

"You're sorry?"

He seemed to be prepared for a lashing as she questioned him. She took her eyes from him to study the way the water moved around her hand.

Olivia nodded and then began to swim toward the shore. She could hear Grey behind her, splashing with his ascent to the beach.

As Olivia walked through the sand, she eyed Morgan sitting at the picnic table closest to the water. When she sat down beside her best friend, Morgan turned her attention away from the flirtatious boy across the table.

"Have a nice swim, Liv?"

Morgan's eyebrows wiggled mischievously as she nodded her head toward where Grey now stood surrounded by a handful of girls.

"You saw?"

Olivia hung her head as her friend placed a hand on her arm in comfort, "Yeah, I was shockingly the only person paying attention to the hot make-out session in the lake. What were you guys thinking? Well, I know what you were thinking… but why now?"

"I have no idea. Something just came over me. I don't know what he was thinking. Morgan, you know how I feel about dating in high school. And if my mom found out…"

Morgan shifted in her seat to face Olivia, "Liv, don't freak out over a kiss. Grey isn't just some guy from high school. He's been our best friend for over a year and never once has he been anything but respectful and kind. Why can't you let yourself be happy?"

"You know why."

"You are not your mom. But you do need to stop letting her control you. She sucks all the happiness from you with one word. Don't let her ruin your life."

Olivia could only nod as a lump in her throat formed, her eyes glancing up at Grey. Although he remained amiable to his company, his eyes kept wandering to where she sat at the picnic table.

All of the doubt, fear, and insecurities ingrained in her from her upbringing came to the surface as they met eye contact.

Olivia turned her attention to the soft rippling of the lake water where Grey and she just kissed, "If he knew what was good for him, he'd pick someone else."

Morgan frowned as she always did when she watched her best friend give up yet another piece of happiness in her life. Only this time, Olivia didn't seem so sure of her decision.

Chapter Ten

"See you guys later. I'll text you tomorrow, Liv."

With another ornery wiggle of her eyebrows, Morgan closed the car door and walked toward the front of her house, leaving only Grey and Olivia in silence.

He put the car in drive when Morgan was out of sight and pulled back onto the road. As they made their way to Olivia's house, Grey cleared his throat and resituated his hands on the steering wheel.

"Are we going to talk about what happened, Liv?"

Olivia stared out the passenger side window at the houses they passed, the glow of the sunset illuminating their roofs with warm hues of orange.

"There's nothing to talk about, Grey."

Why did I have to be so prideful? Talk to him!

He nodded his head and pursed his lips as if he had expected exactly that reply. The rest of the ride to her house was silent save the sound of the cool night breeze blowing through the driver-side window.

Before Liv exited the passenger door, she turned to look at Grey who remained focused on the road ahead of him.

"Grey, I'm sorry."

"Hey, there's nothing to talk about, right?"

When Grey's eyes met hers, she could see the hurt and frustration in his solemn brown eyes. Olivia let go of the door handle and placed her hands on her lap.

"I don't want to lose what we have, Grey. You're one of my best friends..."

"You don't have to explain, Liv. It's fine. I'll just talk to you later."

He returned his attention to the front of the car as if he was finished with the conversation. Irritation swelled in Olivia's chest as heat crept up her neck.

"Greyson, would you stop it? I'm sorry, okay? I don't know what that was at the lake. I don't think either one of us knows what it was. Maybe just something that came over us in the heat of the moment."

Grey hung his head and shook it in disagreement, "Did you ever stop to think that the kiss meant something to me, Liv?"

Olivia sat quietly as he finally opened up and turned his attention to where she sat in the passenger seat.

"I like you, Liv. I have since the first time I saw you walk into church."

"Grey, you know how I feel about dating and you know why. Do you realize that my mom berated me last night when she saw you drop me off? She's probably watching right now."

He looked toward the front window before returning his attention to Olivia, "Yeah, I know about your no dating rule in high school. And that's exactly why I've been okay being friends with you. But I don't know if that's enough anymore, Liv."

"So, that's the only reason we've been friends for the past year and a half? Because you wanted in my pants?"

"What? No! I mean, eventually…"

He stuttered through the most awkward moment of their entire friendship before gripping the steering wheel and clearing his head.

"I promised God that I wouldn't have sex until I was married."

Olivia could tell by the way he flinched before looking over at her that he expected shock or ridicule for his decision. Instead, she just studied the gold ridges of his irises as he waited for her response.

"That's really cool, Grey. Not a lot of people would commit to something like that. Honestly, most of the high school has probably already had sex. Multiple times. No one waits for their soulmate anymore."

"Exactly. I don't want to give myself away to someone I'm not going to spend the rest of my life with. What would my future wife think when I have nothing to give her that I haven't already shared with someone else?"

Olivia glanced toward the front window of her house as thoughts of her mother and father's past ran through her head. Would they still be together if they had just waited? Would they be happy?

Did I seriously have to think about my mom at this moment?

Grey misunderstood her silence and began clumsily trying to backtrack, "Not that you wouldn't have anything to give your future husband if you... if sex was..."

Olivia whipped her head back to Grey as he ran his hands through his hair anxiously. She put a hand up to stop him from further torture.

"Grey, I haven't had sex. You can stop trying to mend my feelings."

He seemed noticeably relieved as his demeanor relaxed but his leg continued to bounce as he waited for her to continue.

"I was just thinking about my parents. If they would have waited until marriage, maybe they would still be together. They would both have careers, maybe live in the city, and mom wouldn't hate me for ruining her life."

"You didn't ruin your mom's life. Liv, you can't think like that."

Olivia muttered under her breath, "Wouldn't be the worst thing she's told me.

Grey turned in his seat to face her directly, "What? What does she say to you?"

Olivia nodded her head, regretting having told another person details about her bitter home life. The last thing she wanted was for someone to interfere and make things worse. Morgan knew Olivia and her mom didn't get along but she wasn't aware of the worst parts.

"Just forget it, Grey. We're not talking about my mom. We're talking about us, about our kiss at the lake."

Although he didn't seem to forget her confession, he put it on the back burner for later discussion. His eyes lightened from their somber darkness as he leaned forward and looked into her eyes.

"Liv, I don't regret for one second kissing you. It meant something to me but if it's going to ruin our friendship, we can forget about it. I don't want to lose you, even if I can't have all of you."

"So, if you're not in it for sex, then what do you want from me?"

"Do you think sex is all there is to dating?"

"To most teenagers, yes. That's exactly why I avoid dating altogether. I will not end up like my mom."

"And I'm not asking you to end up like her. I would never do anything that you don't want to do. All I want is a chance to get to know you on a deeper level. To hold your hand and kiss your lips like I've wanted to do since the first time you spoke to me.

If you just want to be friends, Liv, I will continue to wait until you're ready. But, if you feel the same way I do, then just know that I would never do anything to ruin your trust in me."

"You've been waiting for me? Is that why you don't seem phased by the dozens of girls who flock around you everywhere we go?"

Grey shrugged as if he hadn't thought about the obsessive girls surrounding him daily, "I don't want them. I want you."

Olivia broke their intense stare as a blush warmed her cheeks. While she always thought Grey was cute and felt drawn to him since they met, the same echoing of her mother's words filled her head.

Stop listening to her. You'll never be happy if you don't block out her voice.

"Why would you want me? Grey, choose someone else. There are better girls out there right now who would love to date you. Why don't you choose one of them?"

Grey lifted her chin from where her head hung and looked deeply into her hazel eyes, "There's no one better for me. I want you, Liv."

With her name still on his tongue, he brushed his lips against hers, holding back from a passionate kiss as he had done before. He seemed to be waiting for a response from her.

Olivia sat in battle with herself, fighting between the feeling of ecstasy Grey's lips gave her and the resonating words of her mother telling her she wasn't good enough.

With all of her strength, she pushed her mom's defeating words from her mind and asked herself what she wanted.

And as Grey began to pull away in rejection, she grabbed the back of his neck and kissed him. He tightened in shock before melting into her. As their kiss deepened, Olivia could feel the ache of longing burning in her chest.

She pulled away before she gave into any more buried desires she had hidden from herself. Grey was breathless as he ran his eyes over Olivia's face, both a hunger and curiosity gleaming in the caramel brown of his irises.

"What does this mean for us, Liv? Because if you want me to act as if nothing has happened, I don't know if I can do that now."

"No, I don't want that. But…"

"No buts. Do you want to be with me, Liv? Because I'm crazy about you. We can go as slow as you want, even wait to date until the end of high school. Whatever it takes to make you mine."

"Can we just take it slow for now… see what this is?"

Grey smiled in relief, baring his straight white teeth in a wide grin, "Absolutely."

"And… could we keep it between us for now? I'd like to figure out 'us' without the entire town gossiping. Plus, Morgan has been hounding me since your first day of school to date you and I really don't want to hear her 'I told you so' song again."

It's more of a dance with musical trash-talking.

They both laughed, the atmosphere around them lighter than it had been since their kiss at the lake. Olivia glanced at her house before grabbing the door handle and opening the passenger side door.

"Wish me luck. We gave her a good show tonight."

Grey's cheeks reddened at the thought of an audience to their kissing, "Good luck."

However, as Olivia waved goodbye to Grey from the doorway of her home, she realized the house was silent inside.

As she walked through the kitchen to her bedroom, she noticed her mom on the couch with an empty wine glass in her hand. She was sleeping, likely drunk from drinking all day as she had begun to do on the weekends.

Olivia breathed a sigh of relief as she grabbed a snack from the kitchen and headed to her bedroom for the night. Morgan seeing her and Grey kiss was one thing. She would not have been able to endure her mother's reaction.

For the first time in her life, Olivia was able to think about a moment in her life not ruined by her mother's berating, negative attitude. She would always have an untainted first kiss with Grey that she could remember blissfully.

Chapter Eleven

"You guys are lame. I'm going to the party anyway. I need to get home to pick out my outfit for tonight."

Morgan slid out of the booth at Sandy's Café and headed for the door with one last ridiculous facial expression for her friends. Olivia and Grey laughed when she nearly ran into the busboy as she jested with them from across the room.

"Well, I don't think I'll ever get used to her."

Grey shook his head and chuckled from across the table over his empty plate. Olivia picked at her fries beside her half-eaten burger, "Who could?"

Suddenly, Grey stood from the booth and nonchalantly took the now vacant spot next to Olivia. She eyed the other patrons in the room and raised her eyebrows in question, "What are you doing, Grey?"

He shrugged, plucking a french fry from her plate as he slouched down in his seat to relax, "I wanted to sit next to you. Is that a problem?"

Olivia glanced up at the girls across the room eyeing Grey, wondering if they suspected anything between the two.

"No, I like it… it's just, what if people see us and find out we're together?"

"For all they know, we are just two friends munching on fries together."

"Wrong. You're stealing my fries. Thief. Where do you put all that food you eat?"

"Honestly, I have no clue. Do you have any idea what being a teenage boy feels like? Never getting enough to eat, outgrowing clothes all the time, and, don't forget, turning into a werewolf at night."

Olivia rolled her eyes and took a drink of her soda before twisting her body to face Grey directly, "Do *you* want everyone to know we're dating?"

"We've been together for a couple of months now and the whole time, I've just wanted to put my arm around you and hold your hand and kiss those gorgeous, pouty lips. Did you wear that pink lip gloss today on purpose?"

"No, I accidentally put on lip gloss today. I was walking down the sidewalk and just tripped onto it. Grey, do you know what would happen if people knew about us? All the gossip, rumors, and nosy girls…"

"And why should I care what other people think? All I care about is you and me. What? Are you embarrassed by me?"

"Of course not. If anything, it's the other way around. I mean, just look at that table full of girls over there wishing they were in my place."

Grey took a drink of his soda and glanced over at the noisy table by the front window of the café, "So, you're just worried what other people will think? You don't have any other issue with everyone knowing about us?"

"My mom is impossible regardless. I like you, Grey. I'm just afraid to burst the bubble we're in right now."

He nodded and seemed to contemplate something before turning toward Olivia and grabbing her chin. With all the gentle passion Grey had ever used with her, he pressed his lips on hers and tangled his hands in the back of her hair at the nape of her neck.

There were several gasps from the table across the room as Grey pulled away from Olivia, looking deep into her eyes, "Pop."

"Grey, what were you thinking?"

"I was thinking that limiting our happiness to a tiny bubble isn't fair to either one of us. Are you mad?"

Olivia stole a glance at the table of girls now huddled up and whispering, "No, I'm not mad. Actually, I'm sorry. I shouldn't have made you hide our relationship instead of just being happy. I didn't realize how that would make you feel."

"Don't get me wrong, Liv. I loved being in our little bubble. But more and more often, I'm having to stop myself from showing you affection everywhere we go."

Olivia smiled as she interlaced her fingers with his larger hand and took one last sip of her soda, "Then, let's go."

Grey's eyes sparkled as he slid out of the booth, never letting go of her hand as they walked out of the café together into the summer heat.

When Grey dropped her off at home that night, Olivia was greeted by her mother at the front door. She was still in her clothes from work, her curly hair pulled up into a bun save a few stray tendrils.

"Olivia Larson, what do you think you are doing?"

Her mother stood with her arms crossed and her eyebrows raised in expectation as Olivia jerked in surprise at her mother's ambush.

"Coming home?"

"I thought I raised you better than this, Olivia."

"Well, that's debatable... but to what are you referring now? I'm home before curfew."

Renee tapped her foot on the floor and sighed, her brown eyes darkened with agitation, "I know about you and the pastor's son. My coworker's daughter and her friend came to work today and that's all they wanted to talk about. Said you were making out with the boy at Sandy's Café."

"We were not making out. Mom, you can't believe everything you hear."

"Olivia, tell me the truth. Are you dating the pastor's son?"

Olivia knew there was only so much she could hide from her critical mother, drooping her shoulders in defeat as she nodded her head in confirmation.

"Your father and I told you not to date until after high school, preferably after earning a college degree."

"Yeah, you and Dad also said until death do you part but we all know how that worked out."

Her mom's expression reddened with anger as she stepped closer to her daughter, the back of her hand slapping across Olivia's cheekbone, "Don't you dare talk to me like that, you little tramp! You're the reason he left me. If it weren't for you, we wouldn't have been stuck in this tiny town. We would have followed our dreams, traveled the world, had careers."

Olivia grabbed her throbbing cheek before sending daggers at her mother through watery eyes.

"If you hate me so much, why couldn't you have just kept your legs together in high school? Or maybe used something called a condom?"

"You worthless piece of trash. You're never going to amount to anything in your life and everyone knows it. Do you think dating a pastor's son will save you, make you worth something? Because you're wrong."

The words spewing out her mother's mouth weren't anything that Olivia had never heard before. She had grown up being told the same things as a reaction to her choices. But never before had it been about a boy.

Hatred burned in her chest every time her mom spoke about Grey, wanting more than anything to forever shield him from her venom. He didn't deserve this abuse.

As Olivia turned to walk toward her room, her mother grabbed her forearm with an agonizing grip of her hand, "Don't you dare walk away from me when I'm talking to you. You will not see that boy again. Do you hear me? That church is nothing but bad news. Once they figure out what you are, they'll throw you out."

"Just like you?"

Her mom's sharp eyes dulled as her daughter caught her off guard.

"Yeah, that's right. Grandma told me what happened between you and the church. Little innocent

Renee got booted out for getting knocked up. They didn't want to marry you and Dad. Maybe they felt bad for him getting stuck with you for the rest of his life."

Renee dropped her grasp of Olivia and pointed toward her bedroom door, screaming at the top of her lungs, "Go to your room now! *Now*!"

With a sense of victory, Olivia stalked off toward her room before her mother changed her mind. She knew as soon as Grey kissed her in the café that news of their relationship would reach her mom.

In a small town like Joliet, Indiana, news traveled fast. Especially news you never wanted spread.

Chapter Twelve

"I told you that I'm going to my dad's this weekend, Grey."

Olivia closed her locker and looked up at Grey, now over half a foot taller than her after his most recent growth spurt. It was their senior year of high school and fall was in full swing.

The two of them had remained inseparable all summer, even more so after their relationship became public. Olivia visited her father occasionally during the weekend as she always had. School, friends, and church kept her from visiting every weekend.

Their relationship was still rocky, the level of trust Olivia once had in him now dwindled to an insignificant level. He seemed glad when she visited but, in a way, remained reserved.

"Oh, I totally forgot. Who am I supposed to sit by at church on Sunday?"

Grey grinned down at her as they walked through the hall of their high school together. Her dark hair had grown past her shoulder blades, its soft waves free from a ponytail today.

Grey's hair had also grown, requiring him to push it back every time he leaned forward. Although she teased him about putting it into a bun soon, Olivia couldn't help but watch his bicep muscle flex every time he ran his fingers through his coffee brown hair.

If she had to be honest with herself, this weekend away from Grey couldn't have come at a better time. Olivia cared deeply for him but she couldn't help feeling like they were losing control of their physical relationship.

Both Grey and Olivia had promised God, themselves, and each other that they would remain abstinent until marriage. However, with each kiss, their level of passion increased and soon enough, they wouldn't be able to resist taking it further.

If she had a weekend away to get a hold of herself, maybe she could regain control of her thoughts. A clear head free of hormones is exactly what she needed.

"I guess you'll have to sit alone with your mom then. I'm sure she wouldn't mind holding your hand either."

"Ha. Ha. You think you're funny."

"You don't?"

As they reached the doorway of Olivia's first class of the day, Grey leaned down and planted a tender kiss on her forehead, "Yes, I think you're funny and beautiful and sweet and way too good for me."

Olivia's smile faded as his last statement set in. Her mother's words echoed in her head telling her that she would never amount to anything: a worthless mistake and a burden.

How long would it be until he figured it out? And at what point would he feel like he also wasted his life on her?

"Don't say that, Grey."

His happy expression drooped as he realized the sudden mood change, "What? That you're too good for me?"

"Yes. I don't like it when you say that."

"Why?"

Just then the warning bell for the start of school rang, forcing Grey to leave Olivia for his class down the hallway.

He squeezed her hand and turned to walk away, "We'll talk later, okay?"

Olivia nodded her head but prayed he would forget the topic. She watched for a moment as he walked away, the fabric tight on his broad shoulders.

It was amazing the physical change that a teenage boy underwent merely during their high school years. It felt like only yesterday when she met the lankier, more boyish version of Grey. She thought he was cute then and even more handsome now.

His jawline had sharpened and his clothes fit tighter over the lean muscles covering his body. Although so much of him had changed since she met him nearly two years before, she still saw the slender boy with captivatingly warm caramel eyes.

And though she cared for him more and more each day, a thought in the back of her mind kept gnawing at her happiness. A doubt planted by the people closest to her in life. Would he leave her like her dad, hate her like her mom, or be taken away from her like her grandma?

***

"So, how is school going, Liv?"

Olivia looked out the passenger side window of her dad's truck as he drove into the city. He had picked her up from school that day, helping her to avoid the dreaded conversation with Grey that would have ultimately happened if he had been her ride home.

She wasn't good enough for him and the discussion would only persuade him of the truth. Olivia knew the conversation had to happen. It wasn't fair to Grey to keep him in the dark. She just wasn't ready to say goodbye.

Why couldn't I just let myself be happy?

"It's fine, Dad."

Olivia saw her dad glance toward her in the reflection of the car window. He looked tired, having worked a long shift before coming to pick her up nearly an hour away.

"Just fine? How are your grades? Friends, boyfriends…?"

"What? Are you going to lecture me on sex now, too?"

Ellis sighed as he made a turn toward his small apartment near the edge of the city, "Liv, you don't have to be like this. I'm not trying to lecture you about anything."

"Well, you would be the first parent in my life not to look for every tiny mistake I make."

Her dad parked near the curb in front of his apartment where several other people walked down the sidewalk next to the truck.

"I know what you're going through with your mom, Liv. And I'm sorry about that but you don't have to be so guarded with me. I'm not here to pick you apart."

"Oh, so now you care? Where are you every single day that she spits her venom at me? Better question: how could you leave your daughter with that woman?"

"I didn't want to take you from your life. You have friends, school, church… Yeah, I know you still go. And no, I haven't told your mom. I heard through the grapevine that you were dating the preacher's kid."

Olivia nodded, the last conversation she had with her mom about Grey dissuading her from furthering the topic with her father. Ellis pulled the keys from the ignition and jingled them in his hand.

"Does he treat you well?"

"Better than anyone else in my life."

Her father sighed again, somberly looking out the window of his truck.

"Liv, I cannot begin to tell you how sorry I am. I was going to talk to you about this later but this is as good a time as any. Do you want to come live with me after you graduate? Your mom can't fight me in court if you're eighteen and you love the city…"

For the first time since he picked her up from school, Olivia turned her head away from the passenger side window and directed her attention toward her father.

"You could go to the university here in the city and I have an extra room. I know my place isn't that big but you'd be with me… I just miss you, Liv."

Olivia's chest fluttered with the idea of escaping her mother's toxic grasp. Excitement built inside of her as more reasons for moving came to mind.

"You mean it? I wouldn't be in the way?"

"In the way? Liv, you have never been a burden. I have loved you since I saw you on the ultrasound. You had me wrapped around your finger from your first cry. I know I hurt you by leaving after the divorce. I should've taken you with me. I can't take that back but I'm trying to make it up to you. I see what living with your mom is doing to you. Let me help."

Olivia croaked out her reply as she looked into her father's identical hazel eyes, "Okay."

"Okay? How's the weekend of graduation sound? That will give me time to get you some new furniture and maybe switch my hours around so I can see you more. Can you hang in there for the rest of the school year?"

"Yeah. I've made it almost eighteen years with that woman. I can make it another semester."

"And until then, you can come over every weekend and on holidays. You can choose your bedding and I can buy those chips you like. You still like those, right?"

Olivia smiled as her father became giddy with preparations for her move. She wouldn't allow herself to become too excited, not after she had lost so much in her life already.

Her father helped take her bags into the apartment and guided her toward the spare room. Together, they talked over several ideas on the layout and furniture for her room.

"I'm starving, kid. Are you hungry? There's this place down the street with the best burgers. I'll be right back."

It was then that Olivia's happiness came crashing down. Best burgers... Grey.

She had to tell him she would be leaving at the end of the school year. The conversation she was already dreading was becoming more and more terrible by the minute.

Chapter Thirteen

Olivia took a deep breath before walking into school the Monday after her dad dropped her off. She hadn't mentioned the move to her mom, not wanting the nightmare that was her home life to become any worse.

Her dad had promised to be there when Olivia told her mom and help move her out as quickly as possible. Though Ellis attempted to remain amiable with his ex-wife for the sake of their daughter, there was only so much peace to be had with Renee. Both Olivia and her dad knew that.

As Olivia walked through the corridors of the school with a sense of dread, she searched the faces of her classmates for Grey. When she reached her locker without seeing him, a sense of relief washed over her.

"Hey, you. I missed you this weekend. It's not as much fun holding my mom's hand at church."

Any other day, Grey's voice and humor would have incited a smile from Olivia. Not today. Today was going to be the day she told him about moving at the end of the school year.

Olivia finished grabbing her books and shut the door to her locker, "Hi, Grey."

"Is it just me or is something wrong? What's going on, Liv?"

Grey's caramel brown eyes darkened with concern as he straightened from where he leaned on the lockers and stepped toward Olivia. She wondered how it was possible to miss someone and want to hide from them at the same time.

"Nothing. I got back home late last night and didn't sleep well. That's all."

He nodded but still seemed skeptical of her lack of excitement in seeing him again.

"Okay, well, I missed you, Liv. I guess I'll see you after class then."

Before she could return his affection, Grey turned and walked down the hallway toward his first-hour class. Olivia let out a sigh and proceeded to her classroom, the tension between them now a gnawing ache in her chest.

The rest of the week went about the same. Grey seemed to be giving Olivia space while she made every excuse not to be alone with him, lacking the courage to initiate the conversation. Luckily, Morgan was a great buffer between the two of them.

"Come on! It's Saturday night. I can't just be your third wheel all weekend. I know you became a churchy person but I still like to go to parties. Whatever it is that you need to talk with Grey about, just get it over with. This has been the longest week ever, Liv."

"You're telling me. I just don't know if I'm ready or not, Morgan."

"You're breaking up with him, aren't you? Oh my gosh, Liv! Why would you do that? He's so hot… and sweet!"

Morgan grabbed Olivia's shoulders, perhaps attempting to shake some sense into her. Luckily the noise level at Sandy's was at an all-time high with the Saturday dinner rush so no one overheard her overzealous best friend.

"I'm not breaking up with him. I'll tell you later. Just go to your party."

"Yes! Finally. You know you can come, too. Maybe a drink or two will help your stress."

"No, thanks, Morgan."

Olivia had witnessed an angrier, more hateful mother because of alcohol. She wanted nothing to do with it.

"Okay. I'll talk to you later. Bye, Grey."

Morgan drew out Grey's name as he walked back to the table from grabbing refills on their sodas. He said goodbye to Morgan with a furrowed brow, confused by her peculiar tone of voice.

"What was that about?"

Olivia shrugged her shoulders and watched Morgan prance out of the café, "It's Morgan. You never know with her."

Grey studied Olivia as if he didn't believe what she said. Maybe he had seen the two girls in deep conversation before Morgan left.

Olivia thanked him for the soda before taking a sip of the dark, sweet carbonation and pretending to notice something through the front window of the café.

"Liv, are we going to talk or not? You haven't wanted to talk since you got home from your dad's. Did something happen?"

"Nothing bad happened, Grey. I just haven't been in a good mood lately, I guess."

"I know you, Liv. You're not telling me something."

He's always been able to read me like a book.

Olivia glanced around at the noisy dinner crowd. Every table was filled with customers and the busboys were having to zigzag carefully around the crowd. Sandy's Café was the hot spot for teenagers in their small town.

"Do you want to get out of here? It's getting pretty busy."

Grey nodded and stood from the booth, waving at the staff behind the counter before following Olivia out of the café. They were there a couple of times a week so the staff had grown quite familiar with the young couple.

"Do you want me to take you home?"

Olivia looked over at Grey from the passenger side of his car. His face was vulnerable to the pain she had caused him over the last week. All she wanted to do was kiss the frown lines from his forehead and bring back the glimmer in his eyes. Instead, the words she needed to say would likely break his heart.

"No. Let's go to the park."

"The park? Why? The sun is about to set. There's not a lot of light left."

"That's fine."

Grey seemed unsure as he put the car in drive and drove through town to the park where they had their first kiss in the lake. As soon as they were parked, Olivia jumped out and began walking through the picnic area to the beach.

"Are you going to tell me what we're doing here?"

Grey's voice was not far behind as the cool sand enveloped her toes. She kicked her sandals off and walked to the middle of the beach where she sat with her knees pulled to her chest.

He sat next to her on the sand, overlooking the soft waves of the lake.

"Do you ever regret kissing me that day?"

"What? Of course I don't regret it, Liv. It's one of the best choices I've ever made."

Olivia looked into his soft eyes made warmer in color by the orange of the sunset. The comforting glow of evening illuminated his golden-brown eyes and dark hair. The sight of him was far better than the most colorful of sunsets, the clearest of oceans, the greenest of fields.

At that moment, she had never wanted anything to be hers more than him. He opened his mouth to explain but her lips halted any words that might have been spoken.

Olivia kissed Grey with a hunger and passion they had never experienced during their kissing, a desire surpassing all of their previous temptations.

She heard a soft moan in his throat as the kiss deepened, innately drawing her closer to him. Her head was light as their passion heightened.

Grey's hands traveled up her back and to her hair, his fingers tangling in its long, dark strands. Soon, they were lying back on the sand of the beach, intertwined together.

Olivia's hands hungrily pulled at his clothes but when her fingers grazed the button of his shorts, Grey stiffened. His eyes shot open and he withdrew his lips from hers, "What are you doing?"

"I don't know if you know this but people don't usually stop to narrate."

"Liv, I made a promise… to myself, to my future spouse, to God… to you. Why…"

"Do I need a reason why I want you? Something just came over me."

Grey sat up from lying on the beach, running his hands over his hair to rid it of any leftover sand, "You don't think I've experienced the same feeling? It's not going to be easy but I thought we were doing this together."

"I'm sorry, okay? Can you just take me home?"

Olivia stood up and brushed off her clothes with her hands. She watched as Grey stood up quickly and kicked sand toward the water, "So, now you're going back to being cold to me? What did I do to deserve this, Liv?"

A different kind of fire burned in her chest now, one of anger and pain, "You're right. You deserve better. Why don't I make it easy on you then? I'll find my own ride."

As Olivia attempted to stalk off into the dusk, Grey caught her elbow with his strong hand. She pulled it from his grip viciously and turned on him.

"Don't touch me, Grey. Just leave me alone. If you knew what was best for you, you'd finally date one of the numerous girls chasing you."

"I told you I don't want them. I want you."

Olivia's hands shook as she stood her ground, fists clenched at her side, "No."

"No? What do you mean 'no'? Liv, talk to me. What's wrong?"

"I'm what's wrong, Grey! When are you going to see that I'm not good enough for you? Everyone else sees it."

"That's not true…"

"Do you not hear what people at church say about us? A couple of weeks ago, I was in the bathroom when two older women came in. They didn't know I was there and I overheard them say what a shame it was that the pastor's son was involved with such a sinful girl… and how they know several girls who would make a far more 'suitable' match."

"Why do you care what they think? You should care what I think! I want to be with you, Liv. Isn't that enough for you?"

"I'm not good enough for you, Grey. Please, I'll be fine. Go live your life. Find someone better for you. Find a girl who won't try to have sex with you on a beach and break your promise."

"It takes two, Liv. It wasn't necessarily easy for me to stop. And you're more than enough. You're what I've been praying for my entire life. If you care what others think so much, then know that my parents love you. Please stop this."

Grey extended his arm to grab her hand but was denied when Liv took a step away from him, "I'm moving, Grey."

"You're moving? Where? When?"

"To my dad's apartment at the end of the school year. We decided last weekend when we got to his place. My mom has no idea... but she won't miss me."

"And you didn't think to mention it to me for a week?"

Olivia shuffled her feet in the cold sand and glanced around at the autumn colors filling the surrounding trees. Their beauty was dampened by their topic of conversation.

"We knew this would happen when we both went to college anyway. And I've been trying to tell you but…"

"You've been trying to avoid me for a week. Don't act like I'm stupid, Liv. I've seen it. I thought you needed your space, that something happened between you and your dad or mom."

"I don't want to hold you back, Grey. And I especially don't want to take anything away from a happy future with your wife. I'm so sorry."

"No. I'm not letting you go, Liv. You were made for me. And I was made for you."

"Grey, I'm so sorry. I didn't mean to hurt you. It just took me this long to realize I was taking you down with me."

Grey shook his head adamantly and ran his fingers through his hair roughly. His eyes were glossy when he looked back down from the sky. It was as if he had been searching for answers in the clouds.

He stepped forward, taking Olivia's chin in his hands and kissing her desperately on the mouth. When he pulled away, he rested his forehead on hers and whispered, "Please stay with me. I love you, Liv."

Olivia's heart skipped a beat upon hearing those words for the first time. No matter how badly she wanted to forget their horrible fight, she knew deep down that she was doing what was best for Grey. He deserved better.

"Can you take me home?"

There was a sharp gasp before Grey stepped away from Olivia. He dug in his pockets for his car keys and nodded in confirmation.

It seemed as though he had given up on his pursuit of her as he defeatedly walked up the hill toward the car. The ride to Olivia's house was completely silent save the sound of their breathing.

Without another word, Liv opened the car door and retreated up the sidewalk to her house. Even though she refused to turn and wave as she had always done, Olivia knew that Grey was waiting for her to enter the safety of her home before driving off.

Turn around and run back to him. Tell him you love him.

And as she heard the car pull away from the other side of the entry door, Olivia felt a piece of her go with him. A piece she would never get back.

Chapter Fourteen

"You broke up with him? I've never wanted to slap you more than I do right now, Liv."

Morgan's dark brown eyes were framed by fiery red curls befitting of her sass. She sat across from Olivia in the cafeteria at school the following Monday, ignoring the crowds of other students around them.

"Don't make me feel worse than I already do, Morgan."

Olivia glanced up when she felt a tingling sensation run up her back. She had developed a certain sense for Grey since she had known him, a feeling that coursed through her body when he was close.

Out of the corner of her eye, she watched as Grey walked down the main aisle close to their table and found a seat at a table diagonal from theirs. Morgan raised her eyebrows as she looked between her two best friends, "Wow. Did it get cold in here or is it just me?"

Olivia poked at the chicken strips on her plate and fought the urge to look at Grey again. He hadn't given her the time of day as he strolled by, sitting next to a couple of his friends instead of her. Of course, a flock of girls surrounded his table. He was hot and, thanks to her, single.

"If it makes you feel any better, Liv, he still doesn't look interested in the vultures at all."

Just as Olivia allowed herself one glance in his direction, Grey took his eyes from his plate and stared at her. There was both sorrow and longing in his expression as they locked eyes from across the aisle.

The moment was interrupted when a girl from a grade below tapped on Grey's shoulder. He acknowledged the girl and politely listened to her ditsy rambling. Olivia pushed her plate away as the bitter taste of jealousy filled her mouth.

"You love him, don't you?"

Morgan leaned forward, placing her hand over Olivia's. Although Morgan was mostly energetic and unpredictable, she allowed herself to be empathetic and heartfelt with those closest to her.

As Olivia looked into her friend's big brown eyes, she felt the sting of tears in her eyes just before they began rolling down her cheeks.

"I can't be here right now. Sorry, Morgan."

Grey's eyes were locked on Olivia as she stood and exited the cafeteria. He brushed off the girls vying for his attention and followed her into the hallway, "Liv, wait!"

Olivia spun around as Grey jogged to catch up with her. She attempted to wipe any remnants of tears from her face before looking up at him in anticipation, "What?"

"I saw you watching me in the cafeteria, Liv. That's not something you would do if you didn't want to be with me."

"Well, I don't. So, can I go now?"

The words burned in her throat as she watched the hurt in his eyes.

"You don't mean that. I can see it in those big, beautiful hazel eyes. Why are you pushing me away?"

Grey took a step toward Olivia, the warmth of his body gracing her skin. He wiped a tear from her cheek with his thumb, leaving electricity in its wake.

"I can't do this here, Grey."

"Then I'm giving you a ride home after school. We'll talk then, okay?"

Olivia thought she owed him that much. Nothing made a break-up harder than not knowing why it happened. He deserved to know it wasn't his fault. She nodded and spent the rest of the day pondering how to explain everything to him.

When they got in the car together after school that day, the silence was deafening. Grey, though patient at first, seemed irritated by the time he pulled his car in front of her house, "I thought we were going to talk about this, Liv."

"I'm sorry. We are. My mom is going out for drinks with her coworkers after work. Do you want to come in for a drink or snack?"

"Fine. Just let me text my mom."

Olivia unlocked her front door as Grey placed his phone back into his pocket. When he walked through the entryway, his curious eyes scanned over the entire house.

"That was the kitchen. Through there is the living room. And this is my bedroom."

Grey studied the white furniture, the posters on the wall, and the untidy bed covered in laundry. He stood with his hands in his front pockets, watching her in expectation.

"Let me begin by saying once again that I am sorry. I'm sorry I dated you when I am incapable of loving you like you deserve. I'm sorry I hurt you like I did on the beach. And I'm sorry you wasted your first kiss on someone like me. Grey, you deserve someone so much better."

"Isn't that for me to decide? You can't make that decision for me. Neither can my parents or those gossips at church or our classmates or either of your parents."

"Grey, you don't know what I am. I'm trying to save you from a life of misery."

"You make me so happy, Liv. Happier than I've ever been."

Olivia shook her head, searching desperately for the words to make him understand. Just as she was opening her mouth, she heard the sound of the front door unlocking.

"Oh my gosh, my mom is here. Hide!"

"Hide? Why…"

Grey seemed shocked as Olivia shoved him toward her closet, closing the door just in time for her mom to walk into her room.

She whirled around to witness her mom kick a piece of laundry across the floor with her heel. When Renee stumbled, Olivia knew she had been drinking. Too much.

"Olivia, this place is a mess. I guess you and your room have that in common."

"Hey, Mom. I see you went out drinking with your friends after work."

"Why? Am I not allowed to have a life? Haven't you taken enough from me?"

"No, I just…"

"It's not like I had much to come home to. You ruined my life, my marriage, my body... I should've aborted you when I had the chance before your father found out. He's the one who wanted to keep you. Now where is he?"

Olivia flinched at her mother's confession of wanting an abortion. It made her wonder if it would've been easier that way. If she had never been born, maybe her mom would have been happy.

"You have nothing to say? You're lucky you have some good looks. Maybe you can trap a boy into supporting you the rest of your life because you'll never succeed at anything."

How could you treat your daughter like this, Mom?

Her mother continued to scrutinize her room as Olivia purposefully leaned against the closet door, feeling the pressure behind it as Grey pushed to escape.

If he thought the current conversation was bad, he would be shocked by what her mother would do if she knew a boy was hiding in her closet.

"I'll clean up my room right now, Mom. I'm sorry."

Renee cocked her head sharply and studied Olivia, most likely confused by the submissive tone of her normally insubordinate daughter.

"Whatever. I'm going to take a bath."

Her mom sauntered out of the room in time for Olivia to lose the battle between her and Grey for the closet door. When he busted out, his eyes were wide with shock.

Just as Olivia thought he was going to follow her mom down the hallway, he wrapped his arms around her and held her to his chest. His soft lips pressed against the top of her head before he pulled her away to see her face.

"Let's get out of here, Liv."

"Wait for my mom to start the bath and we'll make a run for it. "

He nodded and listened at the door for the sound of running water. When the coast was clear, the two of them quietly made their way out of the house and into Grey's car parked on the opposite side of the street.

Grey made several turns before parking in a deserted alley. He shut off the engine and turned to look at Olivia with eyes filled with anguish and sympathy.

"Liv, I had no idea. You told me before how bad your mom was but I just thought you clashed heads once in a while."

Olivia shook her head, unsure of what to say. She knew if she elaborated more on the subject, the tears wouldn't stop. The wall she hid her grief behind would crumble and she would be the same broken little girl her mom created years ago.

"Wait..."

She watched as Grey seemed to put all the pieces of the puzzle together, the gears in his head turning until a flash of understanding crossed his face.

"Is that why you told me you weren't worth my love?"

Olivia allowed him to look into her eyes where he saw her broken mess, her feelings of worthlessness, and her fear of loving too deeply.

"I can't be the person you need, Grey. I ruin lives. I break promises. I push people away."

"So, don't push me away. Liv, you have made my life so much better since I met you. You are blunt, hilarious, sassy, gorgeous, compassionate, kind... Don't let anyone else tell you who you are or what you're capable of."

"You deserve someone with a mom and dad who are married, who have a great big Christmas dinner, who will make wonderful grandparents to your children. My dad lives an hour away by choice and my mom…drinks and verbally, sometimes physically, abuses me."

Grey's sorrowful look quickly turned to fiery anger burning in his eyes, "She hits you?"

"There's only been a couple of times. It's when she drinks… and I run my mouth."

"Stop making excuses and trying to rationalize all of this, Liv! You can't continue to live like this. She's not only affecting your home life but now your relationships. You broke up with me because of the lies she has been putting in your head!"

"That was not the only reason I broke up with you. We almost had sex because of me. And I'm moving after graduation."

"Again, it takes two to have sex, Liv. And why do you automatically assume we couldn't make long-distance work?"

"I'm not worth the trouble of long-distance, Grey. It's too hard."

"Stop listening to your mom! Olivia Larson, I want you: your flaws, quirks, mistakes, burdens, insecurities. I want all of it. The good, the bad, the long-distance, the fights, the tears. No matter what comes, I just want you, Liv."

Lord, let me go back to him. Please.

Olivia's eyes welled up with tears as he professed his love for her. His hands reached across the console of the car to lift her chin. He wiped the tears from her cheeks with his thumbs before gently kissing her lips.

She had missed the taste of him, sweet and warm like honey. When he pulled away from the kiss, Grey's eyes were glossy as well.

"I love you too, Greyson James."

It was as if he had been waiting for those words since he first spoke them at the lake. Grey chuckled under his breath, half in happiness and half in relief.

"I never stopped, Olivia Larson."

Chapter Fifteen

The following Sunday morning, Pastor Liam James spoke on the unconditional love of Christ. Grey and Olivia once again sat together, his arm around the back of the pew as if guarding her against the gossips and their malicious whispers.

"Now, Church, I spent years in school studying God's word. I've been a pastor now for over a decade. And I still cannot begin to understand the love that Christ has for us."

There were several amens from the audience as Grey's dad paced on the stage behind the pulpit, as was his custom. He had a charisma and passion about him that didn't leave room for a disinterested audience. Each person clung to his words as if they were the secret to immortality and wealth.

"He sent His Son to die a gruesome death on the cross for *us*. The murderers, rapists, tax evaders… the list goes on. I have a list of my own sins, Church. But don't we all?

And that is what's amazing. He loves every person the same amount. No matter what you've done in life, your level of success and your failures, He died on that cross for you. He knew every choice you would make in your life long before you were born.

It was my face He saw as He lifted his eyes to the heavens and asked forgiveness for the very same people who nailed Him to the cross.

I held that hammer, Church. I put those nails in His hands. It was my sin that put Him on that cross. He could have lived an eternity in paradise with God the Father without pain, torture, and death.

But I'm here to tell you, Church, that it wasn't my sin holding Him to that cross. It was love. Even as He felt the impossible weight of mankind's sin on His shoulders, Jesus loved us. He *chose* to stay on that cross."

Olivia's eyes stung with the heat of her tears as she tightened her grip on Grey's hand. He pulled her closer against his side, rubbing her arm knowingly.

After church, Greyson's mom invited Olivia to their home for lunch, "I have a big crock-pot full of chili ready to eat. Would you care to join us, Olivia?"

Olivia shuffled her feet as she contemplated the offer. She and Grey were still mending what she had broken and talking through plans of long-distance. She wasn't sure getting closer to his parents was the best choice at the moment.

Grey seemed to understand her inner turmoil and nodded his head in reassurance. Diana James, as gentle and patient as ever, stood waiting for Olivia's answer with a smile on her face.

"I would love to join you, Mrs. James."

"Oh, no, sweetheart. Call me Diana."

The three of them made their way through the crowd, greeting several church members before they finally reached Grey's dad at the back of the sanctuary.

Diana rested her hand on her husband's back and whispered in his ear when his conversation was finished.

He planted a tender kiss on her mouth while her head was still tilted up to him.

She blushed slightly when the pastor smiled down at her. Liam watched in admiration as Diana socialized with the members of their church.

Olivia had no idea what the future held but she wanted a love like theirs. All along, she thought marriage soured over time. Yet, seeing Diana and Liam together proved that love never failed. It's the people who did.

***

Grey's house was exactly what Olivia had expected. It was tidy with a warmth only a loving family could provide. Evidence of adoration for their son was everywhere from pictures on the walls to trophies from his childhood on the fireplace.

While his parents set the table, Grey showed Olivia his room down the hall from the kitchen. With curious eyes, she scanned the room for every detail about Grey she could find.

His bed had been made hurriedly that morning, the comforter thrown loosely over the pillows near the headboard. A pair of socks that missed the hamper lay on the floor around the white basket. There was a small desk in the corner of his room with a laptop and papers scattered across the surface.

Yet, most of all, she noticed how much the room smelled like Grey. Over time, his smell had become intoxicating for her. It could make her head light and her heart flutter.

"You're quiet, Liv. What are you thinking?"

"Nothing. You have a beautiful home. And a surprisingly tidy room."

"Well, I have seen your room. Of course mine seems tidy compared to yours."

Luckily for Grey, I hang clothes up now.

Olivia playfully stuck her tongue out at him from across the room. She ventured toward his desk while he remained close to his bedroom door, careful to provide plenty of space for Jesus between the two of them, per his father's instructions.

As she investigated his desk, her fingers skimmed over several papers. The pictures on top were of the lake with a sunset kissing the ripples of the water and a half-eaten burger from Sandy's Café.

Near the bottom of the pile carefully hidden beneath the other drawings were illustrations of Olivia. Grey immediately stepped away from the door when he realized what she had found.

"You weren't supposed to see those."

"What? Why not?"

"They're not good."

Grey shuffled the papers until her drawn face was once again covered with landscapes. Olivia grabbed his hand and pulled it away from the desk, maintaining eye contact as she pulled one of her portraits back out from the pile.

She was amazed at how beautiful he had drawn her. Grey was able to flawlessly duplicate the delicate curve of her jaw and neck and the almond shape of her hazel eyes.

"They're incredible. You made me look so…"

"Gorgeous."

Olivia looked up from the drawing and into Grey's intense eyes. They held a sense of awe as he studied her every feature. Just as the magnetic pull between them was nearly too much, Grey's father stepped around the corner and announced lunch time.

Grey turned and shielded his private art collection with his back while Olivia carefully placed it where she had found it beneath the other drawings. Together, they followed the scent of chili and cornbread to the dining room where steaming bowls sat around the table.

"So, Olivia, what college are you planning on attending next fall?"

Olivia glanced up at Grey who remained focused on the bowl of chili in front of him. She swallowed hard before answering Diana.

"Um, well, my dad lives in Bailey, which is a city just under an hour from here, and there is a college not too far from his place."

"Do you plan on living with him then?"

Grey cleared his throat and asked for the plate of cornbread in an attempt to change the subject that remained sensitive between him and Olivia. However, Diana stayed focused on the conversation and handed her son the plate without missing a beat.

"I haven't decided yet."

Olivia glanced up in time to notice Grey's quick look of surprise. He must not have realized the doubt she now held for her decision to move.

Liam studied the two teenagers before clearing his throat and stirring his chili, "Diana, if I know you, you will be digging out the photo albums after lunch."

"Mom, please don't. I know every parent wants to show their son's girlfriend all his naked baby photos but I'm begging you."

Diana waved away his concerns as she buttered her cornbread, "Oh, Grey, there aren't that many naked photos and they're mostly of your rear end."

"Mom…"

Olivia couldn't help but chuckle at his embarrassment. A small twinge of jealousy washed over her as she thought about the only experience Grey had with her mom. She would much rather have been embarrassed with baby photos than verbally abused.

After lunch, Diana invited Grey and Olivia to sit on either side of her as she shuffled through the photo album filled with photos of Grey.

As Olivia looked at pictures of his adorable round face and big brown eyes, she noticed that she never saw Diana pregnant. In fact, there were no hospital photos of Grey's birth at all.

"How old were you when you had Grey, Mrs. James?"

Diana casually glanced at her husband and then Grey before Olivia looked up from the photo album. Grey nodded his head at his mother in reassurance, "They were both twenty-eight when they adopted me."

The last words of his statement sat heavy in her stomach as she searched for a reply. Grey noticed her awkward silence and smiled at her, "It's okay. We don't tell many people."

Diana had been studying the two of them with the slightest grin playing at the corners of her mouth. The topics of conversation remained light after Grey's confession with much laughter and memories shared among the four.

Later in the afternoon, Olivia stood by the front door with her jacket on, thanking the pastor and his wife for inviting her to lunch. Diana stepped forward and gave her a gentle hug, a comforting embrace only a mom could give.

"Thank you for loving my boy."

She pulled away with misty eyes and smiled before Grey placed his hand on Olivia's back and guided her through the door. He bent for a kiss on the cheek from his mom before pulling the door closed behind him.

Olivia's memory expanded as she witnessed Diana and Liam begin cleaning the kitchen. Liam wrapped his arms around his wife as the bubbles from the dishwater clung to her arms.

She smiled as she gazed out the kitchen window into the bounty of fall colors right outside.

"I think she's the one, Liam. The one I've been praying for God to bring our son."

Chapter Sixteen

Grey turned the key in the ignition after parking the car. He had taken them to the park without saying a word. Olivia didn't mind; it was one of her favorite places in a tiny town like Joliet.

In the spring, flowers scattered throughout the grounds gave the air a sweet scent. The summer was filled with the smell of grilling and sunshine. But fall was her favorite. The leaves, now red, orange, and yellow, illuminated the entire park with bright colors.

As they stepped out of the car, the smell of autumn clung to her jacket as she breathed in its familiar scent. Grey came around the front of the vehicle and wrapped his arm around her. His jacket fit him well, the navy blue accenting the dark waves of his hair.

There was a slight breeze in the air as they made their way to a picnic table just off the beach. The lake's gentle tide washed over the cold sand where several fallen leaves skimmed its surface.

"I know you're dying to talk about it, Liv."

Grey's expression showed both vulnerability and readiness. While she looked out at the water in search of the right words, he studied his thumb cuticle.

"Why don't you just tell me however much you feel comfortable?"

He nodded appreciatively but remained silent for a few minutes.

"My biological mother was fifteen when she had me. Her boyfriend left when he found out she was pregnant. She had no one to help support her."

"What about her parents? Didn't they help?"

The Adam's apple at the front of Grey's throat bobbed with a hard swallow, "They wanted her to get an abortion."

Olivia's eyes misted at the thought of Grey, tiny and vulnerable in his mother's womb. Her mother's words on the desire to abort her daughter clawed at the back of her mind.

"My mother gave birth to me in a small hospital outside of Palm Springs, California, and surrendered me for adoption. She told the agency not to contact her."

Olivia absorbed the shocking information as they both stared at the water where they first kissed. It felt like an eternity had passed since that day.

"Diana and Liam couldn't have any children of their own. They claim that when they first saw a picture of me, they applied immediately. I was two months old before they could hold me for the first time."

"Grey, I'm so sorry. I had no idea."

"You thought I couldn't possibly understand how you felt when your dad left or your mom didn't want you. I know how you feel more than anyone else ever could. That feeling of abandonment, worthlessness... being unwanted."

Olivia wrapped her arms around his waist and buried her face in his jacket. His arms lay around her shoulders, playing with the loose strands of her hair.

"*I* want you, Grey."

"I want you, too, Liv."

It was as if they both needed to hear those words from one another to numb the pain of their pasts. Olivia released him so that she could see his eyes. The caramel tones of his irises were made brighter by the surrounding autumn landscape.

Her eyes landed on his soft lips but a nagging in her mind prevented her from their touch.

"Grey, I think we should talk about what we're going to do after graduation. Before we go any further with this relationship, we need to clear the air."

"Okay. Well, you said there's a college near where your dad lives. I can apply there. We can take classes together, hang out during our free time…"

Olivia waved her hands, using emphatic gestures to emphasize her point, "No, Grey. You could get into any school and you want to go to a small university in Indiana? I won't let you ruin your future like that."

"It's not ruining my future. I never wanted to go too far from my family. This will only be an hour away. I can still come home for my mom to do my laundry."

His humor did not amuse Olivia as she turned to look out at the lake. She crossed her arms to guard herself against the chilly breeze moving through her jacket.

"Hey, come here. You're cold."

"No. Grey, you are giving up an elite college like Yale or Harvard. No high school romance is worth that and you know it."

"But this isn't just some high school romance, Liv. I want to spend the rest of my life with you. Can't you see that? When you broke up with me, I never stopped loving you. Even with a crowd of desperate girls around me, I couldn't take my eyes off of you."

"Grey..."

"No, listen to me, Liv. I don't know how to explain it but I am drawn to you in every possible way. It's been like that since the first day I met you and it will last long after my final breath on earth. I don't want to live a single day without you next to me."

"And what about when you change your mind years from now and you resent me for ruining your life? What then?"

Olivia didn't know if it was Grey's grave tone and steely expression or the cool breeze that sent chills down her back, "I could never hate you."

"Fine. Here's what we are going to do: we are going to enjoy our senior year of high school together and you are going to keep your mind open to better colleges."

"No…"

"Greyson James, if I am as special as you claim, you can attend an Ivy League school and maintain a relationship with me."

Olivia's stomach was as heavy as a rock as she thought about the possibility of her statement. Grey mulled over her proposal as his eyes skimmed the horizon of the lake. Finally, he shook his head in agreement and extended his hand for a handshake.

"Really, Grey? A handshake?"

His ornery grin should have forewarned her of his intentions as he accepted her hand and pulled her from the bench on which they sat. Grey threw her over his shoulder and ran toward the edge of the water.

"No, Grey! It's freezing! Don't you dare!"

The two ran along the cool sand, playfully threatening to throw the other into the frigid water.

Suddenly, the chilly air of that fall day evolved into a far more bitter cold as Olivia was whisked to a new memory of Grey.

"Do you think your dad is going to like me? I know I spoke to him at the funeral but now I'm dating his daughter…"

"Don't be so paranoid. Who doesn't like you?"

Olivia was right. Grey had a natural likability about him. He was amiable to everyone and had a personality that lit up every room he entered.

"Your mom."

Olivia rolled her eyes and took another step up the slick sidewalk toward her father's apartment, "She hates everyone, especially boys who come within a mile radius of me."

Especially the pastor's son.

During their Christmas break, Grey offered to drive Olivia to see her father during the week. With his work schedule, he wouldn't have been able to pick her up from Joliet.

"She still doesn't know I was in the closet that day?"

"Of course not. Do I look like I have a death wish? Anyway, I don't want to talk about my mom. That's one of the main reasons I wanted to take this trip: to get away from her. To everyone else on the planet, Christmas is a joyful time. But for her, it's the opposite."

"You kind of have to feel bad for her, Liv."

"You're joking. Why would I feel sorry for the woman who has mistreated me all my life? What happened to the Grey who was angry that she hits me?"

Although there was a flash of anger in his eyes at her last question, Grey continued with his explanation sympathetically, "To be that unhappy every single day must make a person feel isolated."

"She brought it upon herself. Now quit. We're going to enjoy our visit with my dad."

Grey offered an uncertain grin before straightening his coat. Olivia knocked on the door of the apartment and was answered by her dad in a Santa hat, his dark stubble replacing the usual long white beard.

"Liv! Hey, sweetheart. I missed you. Come on in, both of you."

The smell of the holidays filled the small apartment: the pine scent from the fresh tree in the corner of the living room, the ham baking in the oven, and the cinnamon pine cones Olivia's dad always bought around Christmas.

Olivia kicked off her wet boots at the door and turned to her dad. He stood scanning over Grey with curious eyes and crossed arms.

"Now, let me take a good look at the boy who finally talked my daughter into dating. Ellis Larson."

Ellis offered his hand for Grey to shake with an ornery look in his eye. Olivia knew by her father's mischievous personality and protectiveness for his daughter that this would be an interesting visit.

Grey slipped off his glove and shook Ellis's hand firmly, "Greyson James. It's nice to see you again, sir. We met at Vi's funeral."

"Yeah, I should have known when my daughter threw herself into your arms crying that you were the boy I needed to keep an eye on."

Even with a wink from Ellis, Grey relaxed only slightly. On the drive to the city, he had expressed his desire to impress Olivia's dad. The pressure to do so was making him tense and unlike his usual self.

Ellis excused himself to the kitchen where they could hear him open the oven. An intense smell of ham and yams wafted to where they stood shedding their coats at the front door.

"Grey, relax. You're acting like he threatened your life. Just be yourself and I promise he'll love you."

Olivia squeezed Grey's bicep and smiled reassuringly before stepping into the kitchen with her father and offering a helping hand. In less than an hour, dinner was served.

The small dining table was filled with honey ham, yams swimming in syrup, garlic green beans, buttery rolls, and macaroni and cheese.

"So, Olivia, I received that promotion I told you about."

"What? Dad! That's great!"

Grey swallowed his mouthful of food and nodded to her father, "Congratulations, Mr. Larson."

"Call me Ellis, son. No need to make me feel too ancient. And thank you both. But I thought that maybe while you're here, I can show you a house I was thinking about buying."

"A house, Dad? You mean you don't like this tiny apartment?"

The sarcasm dripped from Olivia's jest and earned a smile from both of the men.

"This was just temporary. I rented the apartment at the last minute after they offered me a job here. It's been long enough. With you moving here in the early summer, I think it's time."

"Well, Dad, I hope you're ready for some pretty high standards. I want my own room overlooking a body of water with a reading nook, swimming pool, and movie theater."

Grey watched the father and daughter banter back and forth, realizing for the first time where Olivia got her easy-going, playful demeanor. They were both quick-witted and sarcastic, making dinner both entertaining and humorous.

When Olivia stood to take the plates, she demanded that both men relax and watch some television while she did the dishes. Her stern look in both their directions halted any debate on the topic.

Once on the couch, the two men sat in awkward silence for the first few minutes of Olivia's absence. They could hear the clanking of dishes and running water in the sink.

They just sat there silent the entire time? Can we fast-forward this memory, God?

"So, Grey, what college are you thinking about attending next fall?"

"Um, I'm not sure, sir. I plan to apply to a couple of Ivy League schools as well as a few universities."

Ellis nodded his head, raised eyebrows evidencing how impressed he was with Grey, "Ivy League, huh?"

Grey glanced back toward the kitchen and then leaned forward in his seat, "Honestly, I was thinking about attending the university here in the city. It's a nice school and I wouldn't be far from home and…"

"And you would be close to my daughter."

Ellis studied Grey's face, now vulnerable to his confession.

"Sir, I love your daughter very much. And, God willing and with your consent, one day I'd like to marry her."

Olivia's father didn't flinch as he kept eye contact with his daughter's boyfriend. Not a word passed his lips as Grey squirmed in his seat.

"After we earn our degrees, of course. I also would want to talk to my parents and Olivia's mother."

"Now, son, that's the last thing you're going to want to do. I like you and my daughter seems to be crazy about you. When the time is right, we'll talk. But there are two things you need to know. Number one, young love, though thrilling, can make you stupid if you're not careful."

Grey wrung his hands in his lap as he listened carefully to Olivia's father, "And number two?"

Ellis stood to join his daughter in the kitchen, his tone gravely serious, "If you want to make my daughter happy, leave her mom out of every detail of your lives."

Chapter Seventeen

Olivia's chest was tight with anticipation for her weekend plans. Ellis had cleared his schedule so he could drive to Joliet and help break the news of the move to his ex-wife.

Both her parents in the same room promised drama and ruthless bickering. Not to mention, they were also informing her mom that they planned to move Olivia's stuff out the very same day.

Ellis was driving down Saturday to help Olivia pack and Sunday was graduation. They would move her possessions the day of his arrival and make the drive back to the city after the ceremony.

Her dad purchased a beautiful home on the outskirts of the city. It had three bedrooms, a kitchen where you didn't have to squeeze past people to reach a plate, and a spacious backyard with a patio.

In the last few months, Olivia had already prepared her room for the move. From choosing a paint color to picking out a new bedroom set, the amount of freedom she had was almost overwhelming.

Grey had been supportive of the preparations to move, even giddy as the time for graduation drew nearer. With their impending separation, Olivia was uncertain of his eager support for her move.

"You tell your mom tomorrow?"

Grey sat across from Olivia at Sandy's café. With the usual Friday night dinner rush, the large room was crowded and loud. The two of them wanted to eat there one last time before everything changed.

"Yeah. Dad should be there in the afternoon and then we'll tell her together. He offered for me to stay with him at the hotel once we pack all of my things."

"Do you really think your mom will be so angry that you won't be able to stay at home Saturday night?"

Olivia gave Grey a look that he had become quite familiar with throughout their relationship. It told him that

Mount Renee was due to explode and Olivia was expecting some burns from the eruption.

"I wish I could be there for you, Liv."

"No, it would only make her angrier. She'll already feel betrayed. She doesn't need another target for her venom."

It killed Grey to see the effect Renee had on Olivia. No matter how badly he wanted to help Olivia escape in the past, all he could do was console her when Renee had broken her once again.

"I understand. Just text or call if you need me, okay? Even if it's just to tell me it's over and you're okay."

Olivia nodded in agreement and plastered an artificial smile onto her face, "Wish me luck."

You're going to need more than luck.

***

"Renee, you have to understand that Olivia is moving closer to the university. I offered for her to stay with me so she wouldn't have to live in one of those tiny dorm rooms with strangers."

Olivia's mom was disheveled, pacing back and forth in the living room. Her frantic hands had created a frizzy mess of her auburn curls and her makeup was smeared around her eyes.

"You both have been plotting against me. There's no way this was a last-minute plan. So, tell me: how long ago did you plan to stab me in the back?"

"Renee, don't guilt Olivia for wanting to move out so she can go to college. She needs an education."

"It's not like it will do any good. She won't ever amount to anything in life. Might as well save a few thousand dollars and not enroll her at the university."

Ellis's eyes widened at the way Renee so openly spoke about Olivia. Although she was far from a loving mother when they were married, her insults had crossed the line into verbal abuse since he left.

"Renee, I will not have you talking about my daughter like that!"

"Oh, now she's your daughter? Where have you been the last couple of years? Off in the city living the bachelor life while I've been here raising *your* daughter. And what do I have to show for it? A knife in the back."

Olivia rolled her eyes and sighed at her mother's theatrics, "Well, now you'll have as much freedom as you always wanted. I'll be out of your hair soon."

"Yeah, does me a lot of good now that I'm in my thirties. Thanks for leaving me some of my life."

Ellis stood and directed his daughter to go pack in her room, "Renee, that is enough! I should have done this a long time ago. All those years I let you walk all over me, let you treat both of us like trash. It's over! Olivia is the best thing that will ever happen to either one of us and now you're losing her... because of the bitter, nagging, miserable person you have made yourself. Not me, not her, you. *You* did this to yourself."

Renee stood speechless for once, though her expression showed no remorse. Ellis shook his head and stalked off toward Olivia's room.

He hadn't made it a step through his daughter's bedroom door when Renee fully reloaded. She stomped down the hall and threw a finger in her ex-husband's face as he stepped between her and Olivia.

"Get out of my house NOW! You are both trespassing on my property. I want you both out right now."

"I paid child support so half of her possessions come with us. You can keep the furniture but we're taking her clothes. Then, it will be our pleasure to leave your property *and* your life forever."

Olivia began recklessly throwing her clothes into a hamper and the boxes her dad had brought. With her parents' bickering fueling her packing, Olivia was never more eager to leave her mother's house.

She desperately searched her room for anything she may have left behind. There was no way she would be able to come back once she stepped out the door.

Ellis looked behind his shoulder as he stood like a wall between Renee and Olivia, his eyes searching her face, "Are you ready, Liv? You got it all?"

"I think so."

Immediately, he picked up the hamper and a box to carry out to the truck. Renee's eyes followed him until his back disappeared down the hallway. Now alone, she burned holes through Olivia with her dark brown eyes.

"You worthless tramp. Of course, this is how you would leave. Running away like you don't owe me anything. Pathetic coward."

Anger swelled in Olivia's chest as she realized there would be no more repercussions for standing up for herself. She stood, eye to eye with her mother, "Why would I owe you, Mom? For all the verbal abuse? All the times you criticized me until I cried myself to sleep at night? How about the incessant nagging and drinking?"

Her mom stood her ground albeit silently as Olivia took another step toward her. She was so close that the smell of her mother's perfume filled her nose.

"No. Let me think some more. How about never letting my friends come over? Or never coming to any events at school? Let's not forget the times you hit me either. Do I owe you for those things, Mother?

The way I see it, anyone can have sex and push out a baby. Just because you had a child doesn't make you a mom. I'm sick of you tearing me apart.

And you know what? When you forced me to stop seeing Grandma, I never stopped. I went to church with her."

"You what?"

"Yeah, and I still am! I've been going to the same church that kicked you out for getting knocked up. For years! How do you like that, Mom? You thought you could take the joy from my life but you never have. You lose."

Renee lifted her hand toward Olivia but the sound of Ellis's stern voice from the hallway stopped her mid-swing, "You touch her, I'll call the cops."

Ellis took a step through the bedroom door and grabbed the last box, putting a hand on Olivia's back to guide her out of the house. With one final glare in her mother's direction, she said farewell to the home where she grew up.

To the bedroom where she had hidden from her mother. To the bathroom where she had desperately cried in the shower for someone to rescue her. To the dining table where she shared many breakfasts with her dad and where he told her Vi had passed away.

As Olivia stood in the front yard next to her father's truck with the passenger door open, she breathed a sigh of relief. Her mother had slammed the door behind them and was nowhere to be seen.

Who's the coward now?

After Olivia climbed into the truck and shut the door behind her, Ellis pulled the truck into the road and drove away from her childhood home. They hadn't made it two blocks when the adrenaline from the moment wore off and sobs overtook her.

With her face buried in her hands, Olivia's body shook as she wept. She cried over her mother's unending abuse and the years she endured in that house. But mostly, Olivia sobbed over what her childhood should have been.

Ellis immediately pulled over to the side of the road and slid over the bench seat, drawing his daughter to his chest, "I'm so sorry, Liv. I didn't know it was that bad. Baby, I'm so sorry."

Olivia didn't care that her phone was vibrating or that she could hear voices passing on the sidewalk beside the truck. Her prayers had finally been answered. She had been rescued. Bruised and battered, yes. But she was free.

Chapter Eighteen

"Hey, you didn't answer my calls last night. I was worried sick about you."

Of all of the blue caps and gowns in the high school gymnasium, Grey still managed to find Olivia before the graduation ceremony began. Her makeup managed to hide some of the puffiness around her eyes from crying most of the night.

"Yeah, sorry. After moving out of my mom's house and getting my stuff into the hotel room, I just passed out. It was a pretty rough day."

"I can imagine. Are you going to fill me in later before you leave?"

Olivia nodded, her eyes stinging as her mind attempted to unbury the painful memories of the previous day. Grey seemed to understand the sensitivity of the subject and returned to his place in line.

With the modest size of the graduating class, the ceremony was quick and painless. Before Olivia knew it, blue caps were flying in the air and Grey's arms were around her.

He picked her up off the ground and planted a kiss on her lips. His smile was infectious as he bent his head down to her level, "We are officially high school graduates, Liv. Can you believe it?"

She smiled as Grey planted another kiss on her lips, "We did it."

As Olivia surveyed their chaotic surroundings, she fought the urge to look for her mom in the crowd. There was a part of her still yearning for her mother's approval, for a mom who loved her and was proud of her. Another part of her wanted to rub in her mom's face that she graduated high school without getting pregnant.

Ellis waved toward where Grey and Olivia now snaked through the crowd of graduates and their families. He smiled and opened his arms for his daughter, kissing the top of her head before looking into her eyes identical to his, "You did it, sis. Congrats, baby girl."

"Thanks, Dad."

After shaking Ellis's hand, Grey was now absorbed in a conversation with his mom and dad. Olivia glanced around the crowd before looking back at her father. He knowingly shook his head in confirmation of her search. Her mom didn't come.

Their silent communication was interrupted by the gentle voice of Grey's mom, Diana. She hugged Olivia around her neck and congratulated her. Even Liam gently squeezed her shoulders before Diana started directing their small posse to the exit doors.

As requested, Grey and Olivia stood taking pictures against the brick wall of the school. By the time they had exhausted every combination of people for the camera, their cheeks were numb from constant smiling.

A familiar voice came from behind them as they stood laughing over some of the worst photos taken, "You all better have room on that camera for one more picture."

Olivia turned and immediately threw her arms around her best friend's neck, "Morgan! Of course, I want a picture with you. I'm going to miss you so much! Promise we can hang out this summer before you go off to college."

"Absolutely, girl. I'll have time between partying and sleeping. My two favorite things. Besides cinnamon rolls… and air conditioning."

She grabbed the bottom hem of her dress and created a breeze for herself. The humidity of the day made wearing dress clothes and graduation gowns intolerable. Olivia took the opportunity to do the same, albeit more discreetly, while Grey was preoccupied with their parents.

"Maybe instead of partying, you can come hang out with me at my dad's house this summer. He has an extra room you can stay in."

"I know what you're trying to do, Liv, but I'm not meant for that churchy stuff. You don't need to worry about me. I'll be fine."

Olivia had tried several times to invite Morgan to church. Yet, there was something in Morgan's life that stopped her from accepting anything to do with God. Olivia didn't want to be pushy so she let the subject go.

She'd always be there for her best friend if and when she needed her.

"Well, text me when you get settled at your dad's place. I'll want to check it out for sure. And don't hesitate to call or text if something big happens. I don't want a repeat of when you were secretly dating Grey and I found out from some chick at a party. Text me *immediately*."

Olivia laughed as she remembered the theatrical show Morgan performed when she spoke to her after Grey's kiss in Sandy's café. There was hand throwing, pacing, and spit flying as Morgan spastically expressed both her excitement for the new couple and disbelief that she didn't know sooner.

"I will text you if something big happens."

"Good. If you don't, I know where to find you... and your little boyfriend, too."

Morgan squinted her eyes at Grey and made an "I'm watching you" gesture before throwing her arms around Olivia for a tight squeeze, "Love you, girl."

"Love you, too, Morg."

And with that, Olivia watched Morgan's bright red hair disappear into the crowd, bobbing and weaving through taller heads than hers.

"I'm only going to assume that was just the standard threatening stare-down I normally receive from Morgan?"

"Yeah, pretty much."

Grey glanced over his shoulder at their parents and nodded toward the parking lot, "You want to grab a burger and go to the park? I already know Sandy's is going to be packed."

"I can't. My dad and I are leaving as soon as we're done here."

"My parents invited him to their house for lunch. I already asked and they said it's fine."

Olivia furrowed her brow as she stole a look at her father, confused that their plans had changed without discussing them with her. Ellis found her eyes and nodded in approval of the new plans, waving for her to go with Grey.

"Okay, but we can't take too long. We still have to get all my stuff and unpack it at his house tonight."

"I'll have you back in time, I promise. Now, will you please just have lunch with me, Liv? A man can only beg so much."

"A man, huh? You graduate high school and you're all grown up?"

"Absolutely."

Grey winked as he pulled his car keys from his pocket and walked toward the parking lot. He gently intertwined their fingers and smiled at her as they made their way through the crowds of people and passing cars.

With a bag of burgers and fries in hand, Grey and Olivia sat at the picnic table overlooking the lake in the park. Early summer had revived the flowers around the grounds, the smell of their soft petals floating down to the sandy beach.

As they enjoyed their burgers, they laughed and joked about moments during their time in high school: the time there was a fight over the last donut or when Grey walked into a door as he watched Olivia walk away.

"I promise you that door was open before I started walking away."

"Yeah, okay. Whatever you need to tell yourself, Grey."

Olivia took another big bite out of her burger and released a noise of satisfaction. Grey smiled as he watched her relish her favorite food, "You know what I want to do?"

Swallowing, Olivia took a drink of her soda before replying, "What?"

"Find the best burger in the world with you."

She gestured to the burger in her hand, "I don't think we would have to look very far, Grey."

"There are so many burgers out there, Liv, and I want to try them all with you."

"I don't know if that's a realistic goal and, personally, I would be worried for our health with that much red meat."

Grey shook his head, both in exasperation and laughter, "Olivia, can you just understand what I'm trying to say for a second?"

Olivia sat her burger down and realized that Grey had become nervous since arriving at the park. His knee bounced up and down while his burger sat half eaten on the picnic table.

"Grey, what's going on?"

His hands were warm as they enveloped hers, "Liv, there is no one else in the world who knows me as well as you do. You know my weaknesses, my interests, my fears, and my past. And I know yours."

"Yeah… What are you getting at, Grey?"

Grey stood and reached into his pocket, pulling out a small ring box. He bent down on one knee in front of Olivia and held her hands in his.

"I love you, Olivia Larson. We both started this life unwanted but I want to spend the rest of it loving you like you've always deserved. Marry me, Liv."

Grey opened the small jewelry box to reveal a princess-cut engagement ring sparkling brilliantly in the sunshine. His warm caramel eyes searched her shocked expression for an answer while a million questions ran through her head.

Just say yes, you silly girl.

"No, Liv, I know what you're doing. Block out all the voices in your head and listen to one. Listen to what *you* want. And before you say we're too young, the only way I could get your dad's blessing was to promise a long engagement."

Grey's teeth shone brightly in the sun as a wide grin passed over his lips.

"You asked my dad?"

"Yeah, we talked for a long time. In the end, he told me you might say no because of the mistakes he and your mom made so young. But then, he said they never loved one another like we do. I… I just couldn't wait to make you mine."

Olivia smiled at the thought of her dad giving Grey his blessing. She searched her heart and finally broke the silence, "Grey, it's going to take a long time to try all the burgers in the world. I hope you're up for it."

Grey's eyes lit up as he stood from the ground and caught Olivia as she leaped into his arms. He bent down and kissed her, his lips expressing all the joy and adoration he felt for her.

As they slowly separated from their kiss and looked into one another's eyes, Grey cupped her chin with his hand and studied every square inch of her face, "Is that a yes?"

"Yes, Greyson James, I'm yours."

And you're mine.

Grey swept Olivia off her feet and spun around in circles, cheering toward the sky in victory as if he had finally found what he spent a lifetime searching for.

Chapter Nineteen

Olivia received the last of the farewell hugs as she stood next to her father's truck in front of Greyson's house. The evening sky was painted with hues of pink and the temperature was cooling down.

Diana and Liam eagerly congratulated the newly engaged couple once again and began walking up the sidewalk to their home. Grey stepped toward Olivia and pulled her into his chest. She was grateful for his warmth as the cooler evening temperature chilled her bare arms and legs.

"I'll call you when I get settled, Grey."

"No need. I'm coming with you."

Olivia took a step back and furrowed her brow in confusion, "What? I'm going to my dad's tonight. It's an hour away. Do your parents know about this?"

"Yes. They're driving to the city tomorrow… with all my stuff."

"Why? Greyson, just tell me what's going on."

Grey ran his hands through his dark hair and looked up to the sky as if to ask for help, "I got an apartment near the edge of the city. It's not too far away from where you and your dad live."

"Please tell me you did not turn down Yale to go to Bailey University."

"I did."

Grey was tiptoeing on the topic which only made Olivia hotter under the collar, "Why are you just now telling me this?"

"I didn't want my choice of attending the local university to affect your decision to marry me. I knew you would think you're holding me back, that the engagement was the only reason I was turning down Yale."

"It is the only reason, isn't it? If it weren't for me, you would be attending an Ivy League college."

"I've prayed about it, Liv. And I'm going to college here in Indiana."

"Don't be stupid, Grey. We can make this engagement work long-distance. It's not like we're planning on getting married in the next couple of years anyway."

"Did you ever think that I don't want to go to an Ivy League college? Bailey University is a great school where I can be close to my family and never have to leave you. A great education without leaving everyone I ever loved. That's a win, win."

"But, Grey…"

"No, Liv. I've made my decision. I've already been accepted and I sign the lease for my apartment first thing in the morning. Your dad is letting me crash on his couch so I don't have to drive an hour so early."

Olivia glanced back at her dad patiently waiting in the truck. By his cautious expression when he met her eyes, he knew about Grey's plans long before her.

A sense of betrayal washed over her as she realized she was the only one in the dark about Grey's decision. Her eyes began to sting with impending tears.

Grey shook his head and wiped an escaped teardrop from her cheek, "Don't cry, Liv."

"I'm so tired of being the person who holds everyone back. You're giving up so much for me. And I'm not worth that…"

He grabbed her shoulders and forced her to look him in the eye, his serious expression demanding her full attention. Even when Grey took charge, Olivia never felt in danger. In his anger and frustration, he remained gentle with her.

"I don't want you to ever say, or even think, that you're not worthy again. Do you hear me?"

Olivia nodded her head in agreement even as her mother's venomous criticisms cut through her thoughts. She wondered if there would ever be a time when her mother's voice didn't haunt her decisions.

"I'm gaining far more by staying with you, Liv. I love you so much."

Grey kissed her lips softly before opening the passenger door of her father's truck. Ellis smiled as his daughter climbed onto the bench seat and buckled her seatbelt, "You ready to go home, sis?"

She wiped the tears from her eyes and inhaled deeply, "You have no idea."

A content sigh escaped Olivia's lips as the most important men in her life chuckled in unison. Grey ducked his head into the truck and kissed her on the forehead, "I just have to grab my bag from inside and say goodbye to my parents. I'll see you soon. Leave the heavy boxes for me, okay?"

The truck engine revved to life and Grey carefully closed the door, pressing his hand against the window. She mirrored his movement, lining her fingers up against his much longer ones.

Just then, Olivia's memories were thrown into forward motion. The sudden change was alarming and it took longer than normal for her vision to once again focus. Her gaze was still on Grey's hand. However, now she stood clutching it by her side.

Wait... where are we?

Grey's voice broke through the fog in her memories as her surroundings sharpened around them, "Excuse me?"

The usual calm, sultry tone of Grey's voice was replaced by one of surprise and irritation. Olivia searched his face as he stood eye to eye with a professor at the university. Class had just been dismissed and the last few students filed out into the hallway.

Olivia nearly flinched as the whiny voice of their professor hit her ears, "I was just giving a little friendly advice. I see the way you distract one another during class. Perhaps you could focus more if you prioritize your studies over your relationship."

I always hated this professor. I'm not sure what was worse: his nasally voice or his condescending attitude.

Grey shifted his stance so that he created a protective wall between Olivia and the negativity of their professor, "With all due respect, sir, we both have A's in your class. And, not that it's any of your business, but if I want to look at my gorgeous fiancée, I will stare at her whenever and wherever I please."

"Fiancée? You are more foolish than I had imagined. Far too young to know anything about a real relationship. Your education will last longer than this infatuation."

Olivia noticed the tension in Grey's shoulders and pulled his forearm to lead him out of the classroom. His skin was warm and taut around his thick, muscular arm. Although Grey remained calm in most situations, he was fiercely protective of those he loved.

Stiff as a board, Grey turned toward Olivia and guided her out of the classroom with a hand to the small of her back. Just as they were nearly in the hallway, Grey stopped dead in his tracks and returned his focus on the professor who had begun erasing the chalkboard.

"We'll just have to wait and see if you're wrong, won't we?"

Now outside in the courtyard, the early spring breeze sent a chill up Olivia's arms. Grey pulled her closer to him, the heat from his side radiating through her jeans and loose-knit sweater. After knowing one another for five years, he recognized what she needed without a word.

"Are you okay, Grey?"

He shook his head but his lips remained pursed as he attempted to calm down from the intrusive professor.

"Don't listen to him, okay? He doesn't know anything about us or what we've been through together."

Grey's eyes were dark as he tilted his head down to study Olivia's face, "You mean it didn't scare you when he said we were too young?"

"No, he's just an arrogant jerk. Wait… did it scare you?"

Olivia's chest tightened with the thought that Grey was doubting their relationship. Her life was going so well lately. It seemed right that something would go wrong.

Her fears dawned on Grey as he stopped mid-stride on the courtyard sidewalk and wrapped his comforting arms around her shoulders, "No, Liv. He didn't make me question us. I thought he scared you away. I know you don't want to repeat your parents' mistakes…"

"We're not being stupid about this, Grey. It's not like we're rushing into anything. And I don't know about you but I'm enjoying being engaged to my best friend."

They continued walking down the sidewalk toward the parking lot to Grey's car. Olivia smiled up at him as their fingers intertwined and he returned the sentiment, "I am, too. But…"

"But what?"

"There is a part of me that can't wait to be married to you, Liv. I hate saying goodbye every night and staying in that lonely apartment by myself. It would be a much better place if you were there with me."

"Get your mind out of the gutter, Greyson James."

Grey's deep chuckle filled the silence of his car as they both buckled their seat belts, "There is no shame in wanting to cuddle with your wife at night."

"Cuddle, huh?"

Olivia playfully punched his arm before glancing at the time on the dashboard, "We better get going. My dad is waiting on us for dinner."

Grey put the car in gear and made his way through the traffic and pedestrians. His brow was pulled together in deep thought before he abruptly broke the silence.

"Are you not attracted to me, Liv?"

Her eyes widened in shock. Olivia studied Grey as he made a left turn out of the university parking lot. Since high school, he had filled out nicely. No longer the lanky boy she first met, Grey's button-up shirt and jeans tightened around his flexing muscles.

The gold of his eyes remained unchanged; the familiar warm caramel brown never ceased to offer comfort in times of distress. His hair was shorter than in high school, the dark waves tamed close to his head.

With a sharp jawline, slightly tanned skin tone, and soft lips which begged to be kissed, there was nothing about Greyson James that Olivia did not find attractive.

He gets more handsome every day.

After more than enough time taken to study his features, Grey glanced over at his silent fiancée from the driver's seat with one hand on the wheel, "Is that a no?"

"No, I definitely am… I just…"

"Just what?"

"I just don't want us to go too far and break up again. My life is going well. Almost too good to be true. I feel like something bad is going to happen and I don't want it to be us breaking up."

When Olivia usually became anxious about a topic, she would repeatedly wring her fingers in her lap. Grey reached over the console to still her fidgeting, rubbing his thumb over her knuckles.

"That will never happen. I'm sorry. I really do appreciate the precautions you've been taking. I just feel like I'm going to explode and you seem so calm."

"Believe me, it's not easy."

"Can I ask a favor?"

"Anything."

"I know the weather is getting warmer and it will be time for you to wear your little dresses, shorts, and tank tops. But could you only wear my favorite dress when we're with your dad? He can act as a sort of buffer."

"Your favorite dress? I didn't know you had a favorite."

"Strappy, black, lacy… Please, anything but lace."

Olivia burst out laughing at the torment in his voice over something so simple as the material of her dress. It would certainly be a challenge for them to maintain their promise of purity. But anything good was worth waiting for.

And Greyson James was definitely worth the wait.

Chapter Twenty

Olivia and Grey sat at her father's dining table addressing envelopes to their wedding invitations. Soft music played in the background and their empty dinner plates sat on the kitchen counter.

"Don't forget to send Morgan's invitation to her new address. She moved back from California when she graduated. Hopefully, she'll get that job she interviewed for in the city."

"Are you kidding? It's Morgan. You know she won them over instantly."

Olivia smiled as she thought of her best friend whose bright red hair matched her vibrant and infectious personality. Over the past four years of college, they had kept in touch, taking trips at least once a year to see one another.

Morgan majored in English and journalism, eager to earn a position at a woman's magazine. Unsurprisingly, she hoped to provide blunt commentary on issues such as women's rights, sexual health, and mental well-being.

Of course, Grey's brilliant mind and amiable disposition had already earned him a position at a local software company contingent upon his graduation next month.

Olivia was still searching for a job in her field. Alongside Grey, she would be receiving a bachelor's degree next month. Except, instead of computer science, her major was in child development.

When she decided on her major, she prayed to God to reveal what she should do with her life. After what felt like months of unanswered prayers, her psychology professor lectured on child development and the impact of one's upbringing on their adult life.

It was as if God had tapped on her shoulder and nudged her toward a career as a social worker. She wanted to help children who endured both physical and mental abuse like she had growing up.

Even if she couldn't change her past, maybe she could help change another child's future. She wanted to make a difference, not sit behind a desk for the rest of her life. If only she could get a job.

Just then, Grey interrupted her train of thought as he held up a blank envelope, "Liv, are you going to invite your mom?"

A twinge of pain passed through her chest at the thought of inviting her mom to the wedding. Olivia hadn't spoken to Renee since the day she moved out of her childhood home.

"I don't think she would come."

Grey dropped his focus as he manipulated the corner of the envelope between his thumb and index finger. Though he nodded in understanding, his expression showed the subject wasn't totally closed.

"Can I speak openly?"

Olivia pulled in a deep breath and looked into his darkened irises, "Don't we always?"

"No matter what she's done to you in the past, she's still your mom. I think you would regret not inviting her to your wedding."

"Do you think I want to spend my wedding day listening to her criticism or being judged with her smug expressions? I don't want to feel like I'm not good enough on my wedding day."

"Liv, you haven't spoken to her in four years. Maybe she's changed. Maybe she realized how much you mean to her since you've been gone."

"She had eighteen years to realize how much she loved me. Or how much she should have."

"Forgiveness is a hard thing to give, Liv, especially to the people who hurt you most in life. But God did not create us to harbor hatred. The bitter feelings you hold for her are only hurting yourself."

Olivia shook her head, every vicious criticism and slap replaying in her mind over and over again. How could God want her to forgive the person who abused her for the majority of her life?

"I can't, Grey. Not after all she's done to me. Why can't we just be happy on our wedding day?"

"We will be but…"

"No, we won't. Not if she's there. That's what she does. She sucks all the joy from your life until you're as hopeless and miserable as she is."

Grey tossed the blank envelope onto the table and pushed his chair back, crossing his arms over his chest, "I know it's hard. I never thought I would forgive my biological parents for the choices they made. But I realized I could never be truly happy in life if I still held onto my past. You can't move forward if you're still clutching all that heavy baggage."

Olivia sat miserably stewing over images of her mother as Grey stood from the table with their empty glasses, "I'm not forcing you to do anything, Liv. Just think about it."

She looked down at the blank envelope in front of her on the table with a pit in her stomach. After years of loathing her mother, it felt impossible to forgive and invite her back into her life.

Since she left four years ago, her life changed for the better. After escaping abuse, everyday struggles seemed menial compared to the treatment she had previously received.

When Grey sat down at the table from refreshing their drinks, he picked up the envelope Olivia had finished filling out. Alongside the address of her childhood home were wet spots from tears shed as she let go of the hatred which had poisoned her since childhood.

He dropped the thick, crème-colored paper and opened his arms in offering to his fiancée. Olivia stood and immediately fell to her knees, sobbing over the pain she had relinquished to God.

Grey's arms wrapped around her as her body shook in sorrow. His lips pressed against the top of her head as he pulled her onto his lap and rocked her in comfort, "It's okay, Liv. It's over, baby, it's over. You did it."

***

The wedding took place in the small church where Grey and Olivia first met. The warm spring air lifted the fragrance of the flowers around the church, surrounding family and friends who had come to witness their union.

Pastor Liam James stood by his son with a tearful yet proud expression on his face. His mother sat in the front row with a tender smile and misty eyes.

Olivia took a deep breath as she watched Morgan disappear behind the sanctuary door to walk down the aisle in her pastel yellow bridesmaid's dress. Her bright red hair was pulled up into loose tendrils and her makeup illuminated her gorgeous brown eyes.

When Grey's cousin offered her his arm, Morgan had given Olivia a wiggle of her eyebrows at the handsome young man.

There was no mistaking his good looks; his green eyes and blonde hair were striking in his gray suit. Grey hadn't hesitated for a moment in choosing his childhood friend and cousin to be his best man.

The end of the first song could be heard through the lobby doors. Olivia looked up into her father's eyes, a bittersweet mixture of emotions filling his eyes so similar to her own, "I feel like I just got you back, Liv. Now, I have to give you away."

"You never lost me and you never will, Dad."

He dropped his head as he clasped her hands, a shaky grin passing his lips, "I never thought I would be able to say this but... he deserves you."

Olivia nodded in agreement and thought of how handsome Grey must look in his charcoal gray suit surrounded by white flowers on the stage. They had waited four long years since their engagement for this day and now that it was here, it still felt like a dream.

As the doors to the sanctuary opened, the audience stood and watched the bride and her father walk down the aisle. Olivia's eyes automatically found Grey's. His golden eyes lit up at the sight of her, an expression of awe and utter joy that caused butterflies to fill Olivia's stomach.

White delicate lace wrapped around her arms and chest, flowing down to the train behind her. Her long hair was woven together into a loose braid down her back. Small white flowers peeked out of the tendrils in several spots.

When they arrived at the front of the church, Grey tore his eyes from Olivia and hugged Ellis around the shoulders. Her dad clapped his back and offered Olivia's hand to him, "Take care of my heart, son."

Grey nodded in agreement and returned his eyes to Olivia's, "Yes, sir."

He flashed his teeth in a wide smile as he led her to the altar, never once taking his eyes from the sight of her.

Pastor Liam opened his Bible and began the ceremony, "Today, I have the honor of not just marrying two people who are very much in love, but my son to his soul mate. Their journey began seven years ago when they were only fifteen years old. I remember the day Grey first saw Olivia. He couldn't stop talking about how beautiful and vibrant this young woman at church was. Little did I know how much Olivia would remind me of her grandmother, Vi Larson. Her sweet and kind soul gently washes over you only to be brought quickly back to reality with her sharp wit and honest commentary."

Olivia's eyes stung with tears as she looked over at the table to the side of the room with her grandmother's picture and tealight candles. She glanced at her dad where he sat in the front row. Ellis nodded his head, approving of the similarities between his daughter and mother.

When she returned her focus on Liam, Grey still stood at attention, soaking in every word his father spoke,

"God calls us to love one another… in sickness and in health, through mistakes and heartbreak, during the darkest nights and hardest fights.

He calls men to love their wives as Christ loved the church, to protect them, to provide for them, and to remain faithful. And to women, God commands you to respect your husband, submitting yourself fully to him in love and faithfulness.

Now, I could speak on the countless scriptures God has given us on the topic of love but there is no better way to express the love of these two individuals than to hear it in their own words. Son, I believe you've written your vows?"

Grey nodded and turned to Olivia, pulling a small triangle of paper from the pocket of his pants. He inhaled deeply as he unfolded the paper and read his handwritten words, "Olivia Larson, I promise to love you every second, minute, and hour of every day for the rest of our lives.

I vow to never take you for granted, to always choose you first, and to always be thankful for the gift you are to me. All my life, I've prayed for my soulmate but here I stand still in awe of how much God surpassed every single desire. I love you, Olivia. I always have and I always will."

Please, God, just let me hold him.

Grey turned the paper around for Olivia to see. There on the crinkled notebook paper was an animated hamburger and milkshake, worn from being drawn years prior. At the bottom of the page beneath their drawings were Grey's handwritten vows.

Olivia smiled through tears as she realized he'd kept their first note from high school. She swallowed hard, pushing past the emotions that tempted to overwhelm her voice. Then, she accepted her written vows from Morgan and turned back to face Grey.

"Greyson James, I vow to always appreciate your tender and generous soul, to love you unconditionally, and to always follow wherever you may lead. You are my comfort, my best friend, and my joy. There are not enough words to express how much I love you so I'll just have to start with the two most important words I'll ever mutter: I do."

Liam's smile rivaled the bright afternoon sunshine streaming through the windows as he glanced between the bride and groom. Grey gently pushed the wedding band onto Olivia's finger just as she had done for him.

"Son, you may now kiss your bride."

Greyson took no time to cross the small expanse between him and Olivia, cupping her chin in his hands. His lips were all at once slow as if savoring the moment and quick as if he had waited a lifetime to kiss his wife.

When he pulled away, his eyes exploded with countless emotions running through his mind: joy, disbelief, awe, and desire.

"May I introduce to you all for the very first time, Mr. and Mrs. Greyson James!"

The applause was enough to shake the entire church as cheers resounded through the sanctuary. At that moment, as Olivia smiled up at Grey and walked down the aisle through the flamboyant celebration, she wasn't thinking about who hadn't come to the wedding or if she was good enough.

For the first time in her life, she felt complete. She wasn't the lonely, desperate little girl whose mother told her she would never amount to anything or the angry teenager who felt abandoned by her father.

No, she was a friend, a beloved daughter, a wife. And as she gazed into her husband's golden-brown eyes and kissed his warm, soft lips, Olivia knew without a doubt that God had created them for one another.

Chapter Twenty-One

"What did you just say?"

"I said I'm pregnant."

Two years after the wedding, Olivia stood in the doorway of their master bathroom with a pregnancy test in her hand. Grey sat on the edge of their bed, his face turning from surprise to utter happiness.

He stood from the bed and swept Olivia into his arms, picking her up and kissing her firmly on the lips. When he sat her gently back down on the floor, he placed his hands against the bottom of her stomach, "We're having a baby?"

"I can't believe it. We haven't been careful for months. I just thought we would have to try harder."

Grey studied her face as he cupped her chin between his thumb and forefinger, "You're happy, right? I mean we talked about this. You were finally getting settled at work and I just got promoted. We have the house, the backyard, the spare bedroom…"

"Yes, yes, I'm happy. I guess I'm still in shock. I'm pregnant, Grey!"

A smile broke across Olivia's face as she threw her arms around his shoulders. Her feet dangled above the soft carpet as Grey wrapped his arms around her and buried his face in her neck.

But like many moments in her life, there was a voice in her head she could never rid herself of. Though she had forgiven her mother for the abuse she endured for most of her life, her absence at their wedding two years ago still left a gnawing in her heart.

Ignore it. Just be happy. Let Grey be happy.

Grey seemed to sense the change of mood and separated himself from Olivia, searching her eyes for a reason for the tension.

"Grey, what if I do the same thing my mom did? What if I screw up our child like my mom did me?"

"Don't say that, Liv. You are nothing like Renee. You are going to be a great mother."

"You don't know that. She was happy until I came along. Then, she felt trapped... like I ruined her life."

"You know that's not true. A child is not the end of your life but the beginning of an extraordinary journey. An adventure we are going to have together."

"What am I going to do about my career? I feel like it's only just begun and now I'll have the baby and maternity leave and..."

His large hands covered her shoulders, "Liv, calm down. It's going to be fine. God will provide."

"How can you have so much faith in God when so much in life still goes wrong? He let my mom abuse me for years, He let my dad leave, and He took Grandma from me, the only person who was there for me at the time..."

Grey pulled Olivia down on the bed with him and tucked her against his chest, resting his chin on the top of her head, "God never promised bad things wouldn't happen in life but that He would hold you through it. Through life, we will lose loved ones, be mistreated and abandoned... but we are never alone."

"All those years of abuse, when Grandma passed, I did feel alone. That's why I chose to become a Christian… but the faith you talk about, I don't have that. Why would the God who spoke the universe into being care about what happens to me?"

"Because He is our Father and He loves His children. I know it's hard to fathom. I don't know if we as humans could ever truly understand the depth of His love but He gives it nonetheless."

Olivia breathed in the scent of Grey as she slid her hands from his chest to his jawline. He tilted his chin to look into her eyes as she placed a tender kiss on his lips.

"Tell me more."

She returned her head to Grey's firm chest and listened to the deep murmur of his voice as they lay intertwined, hands overlapping on her stomach.

***

Four weeks later with their sonogram pictures in hand, Olivia and Grey shared the news of their pregnancy with Ellis. In recent years, his dark hair had gained a handful of grays. However, the slight salt in his pepper hair only made his handsome features more distinguished, something his girlfriend, Audrey, seemed to appreciate.

If Olivia had to admit, it was strange seeing her dad with another woman besides her mom. To add to the oddity of the situation, Audrey was nothing like Renee. She was a gorgeous, petite woman. Her Hawaiian descent gifted her with wide brown eyes and warm brown skin.

Yet, it wasn't merely her appearance that contrasted her mother but her personality. Audrey was relaxed, bubbly, and generous. At family dinners, she was always the first to offer help and the last to place judgment. Perhaps, all in all, Audrey was the perfect fit for her dad.

Olivia liked Audrey very much, which made being happy for her dad even easier.

As she passed Ellis the sonogram pictures and waited for a response, Olivia's stomach fluttered with butterflies. Telling someone outside of her and Grey made the situation so much more real.

Her dad studied the tiny peanut shape and the text on the top of the photo before a wide smile broke across his face, "Olivia James, am I going to be a grandfather?"

She nodded in confirmation as he stood from his black leather recliner and pulled her into his open arms. His deep voice vibrated against her cheek as he chuckled, "My baby is having a baby."

His eyes were glossy as he broke away from their embrace and offered a hug to Grey, a firm clap on the back for the father-to-be, "Congratulations, son. About time you made me a granddaddy. The way you guys rushed off from the wedding reception, I thought I'd only have to wait nine months."

Oh, my gosh. I forgot he said that.

Olivia playfully slapped her dad's arm, her cheeks flushed in embarrassment, "Dad!"

Grey added to the conversation as he pulled Olivia under his arm, "Hey, we waited years before the wedding. That was more than enough for me."

Now it was time for Olivia to nudge Grey in his side, earning a small grunt from her ornery husband. Ellis laughed at his feisty daughter, "Well, we have to celebrate. How about we grill out tomorrow? Or do you already have Saturday plans?"

Grey gave Olivia a knowing look before taking a seat on her father's couch. He ran his hands through his dark waves as he often did when he was anxious.

Olivia sat next to him and cleared her throat, "Um, well, that's another thing I wanted to talk to you about."

The smile faded from Ellis's face as he returned to his recliner, leaning forward with his hands clasped, "Don't scare me like this, sis. What's going on?"

"Ever since I found out I was pregnant, I've felt like I needed to make things right with Mom."

"Liv..."

"No, just listen, Dad. I know she hasn't talked to me since I moved out and she didn't come to my wedding but..."

"But what? Do you think she's changed over the last six years? Why would you want to bring that woman back into your life after so long? Especially now. Do you want your child to be treated like we were?"

Olivia drew in a deep breath before continuing. She had known this conversation would be difficult. Her dad was the only other person who knew exactly what it was like to be mistreated by Renee.

"I've thought it through, Dad. I can't be the mother I need to be if I have this heavy weight on my heart from my mom. I want to make things right."

"Liv, I can't force you to stay but I will not support your choice. Nothing good will come of this."

"God called us to love and I haven't shown my own mother that kind of love and forgiveness. Maybe if I can't get through to her, He can."

Ellis rubbed his eyes before letting his hands fall in his lap. After a moment of silence, he nearly whispered, "Do what you need to do, sis."

Grey rubbed Olivia's back as she stared down at the ultrasound pictures in her lap. There was no doubting the nagging feeling in her chest to make things right with her mom. If not for herself, then for her unborn child.

Ellis's voice broke her concentration on the tiny arms and legs in the photo, "How about Sunday, then? Greyson, we can use my new grill. I've been dying to test it out. Does steak sound good?"

"Absolutely. Can't wait. It'd be great if Audrey could make it. We missed her at dinner last week."

"Yeah, something came up at work. She told me to apologize to you both for missing dinner. I'll mention the cookout to her tonight."

As the two walked out to the backyard to bond over her dad's sophisticated new grill, Olivia returned her attention to the photos on her lap.

Ever since their first appointment at the doctor's office, she hadn't been able to keep her eyes off the tiny figure of her baby.

As tears dropped onto her jeans, she prayed to God to be with her during tomorrow's visit with her mom, "Let Your will be done, Lord. Not my will, God, but Yours."

Chapter Twenty-Two

"Promise me that you will call if you need help, Liv. I will be there as quickly as I can."

"I'll be fine, Grey. Enjoy the afternoon with your parents. I'll be back before you know it."

Grey's brows were furrowed. After nearly a decade together, there was no hiding her anxiety from him with false optimism. He knew her stomach was in knots; the dark bags under her eyes were evidence of her lack of sleep the previous night.

"I'll be praying for you, Liv, and waiting by the phone if you need anything."

"Thank you, Grey, but don't let this ruin the time with Diana and Liam. Let them celebrate with you without any burdens."

Grey nodded his head, glancing back over his shoulder at the front of their house. His parents had been over for brunch when the announcement of their grandchild was given.

They had been overjoyed, giving a plethora of congratulations and hugs to the expecting couple. Diana had cooed over the ultrasound pictures and Liam requested to pray over the newest member of their family.

As always, his passion and adoration for God resulted in a heartfelt and tear-inducing prayer. There was not a dry eye in the house after witnessing a fraction of the conversation Liam James had with God regularly.

In a way, Olivia was envious of the intimacy of Liam's relationship with God. His prayer was not a request to a powerful deity but a dialogue between a loving son and Father.

After spending the entire morning with the pastor and his wife, Olivia stopped procrastinating on the task before her. She knew it was time to go see her mom.

Now, as she stood by the car, the weight on her heart returned in a painful rush.

"Tell them again that I'm sorry to leave during their visit. Invite them to the barbeque tomorrow. My dad would love that."

Grey nodded and bent his head to kiss her lips one last time before she left, running his palm against her stomach, "I love you both. Be careful."

"Are you kidding? Careful is going to be our child's middle name."

Olivia laughed as she climbed into the driver's seat of their car, her hands gripping tightly on the steering wheel. Grey smiled half-heartedly as he closed the car door and waved from the curb.

Now alone in the car, she softly muttered, "It's just you and me now, kid. There's something I need to do for us."

The worship music over the radio was the only reason Olivia was able to pull the car to the curb in front of her mom's house. Though every cell in her body shouted to turn around, the pulling on her heart helped her forge on.

It wasn't until her eyes studied the front of her childhood home that the doubt in her mind began to take over, "God, let Your will be done."

She closed the car door and made her way up the sidewalk to her mom's house, taking a deep breath before pressing the doorbell.

After a moment, Renee appeared on the other side of the screen door. Her face displayed shock before hardening to its usual expression.

"Hi, Mom."

"If you've come to take more from me, you can just leave."

"I just want to talk. Please."

Renee opened the door and allowed her daughter to walk into the living room. The home was slightly different with small updates here and there. Her mom had replaced the couches with a fluffy sectional and the pictures on the wall were no longer of Olivia but landscapes and vintage wine bottles.

They sat on opposite ends of the couch and stared at one another in a long silence before Olivia cleared her throat, "How have you been, Mom?"

"What? Since you left me six years ago? After I pulled the knife out of my back, I was much better."

Olivia stepped around the negativity of her mother's answer and attempted to keep the conversation positive, "Do you still work at the insurance office here in town?"

"Yes. There's not much else I can do without a college degree. Instead of an education, I had a baby."

"Mom, could you please stop attacking me? I didn't come to fight."

"Why did you come then? All you've ever done is take from me. What am I supposed to think of your sudden reappearance?"

"I'm pregnant... and I wanted you to know."

"Well, it happened a lot later than I thought it would. Do you know who the father is?"

Not even a second of hesitation.

Olivia sat with her mouth open, somehow still shocked by her mom's lack of enthusiasm for her grandchild. She gathered herself and answered her mother, her voice hoarse with increasing emotion.

"My husband, Greyson. He's the pastor's son I dated in high school. We're married now. But you knew that from the wedding invitation I sent you."

"Oh, yeah. I saw the envelope was addressed from you and threw it out without opening it."

The pain building in her chest was becoming harder and harder to ignore.

"Yeah, well, it was my wedding invitation. I thought you would want to be there for your daughter."

Her mother shrugged and studied her nails with more interest than she was giving her daughter. Then, something snapped inside Olivia. Perhaps, it was the misery from years of abuse or the protective nature she now held for the tiny unborn life inside of her.

"I don't know why I came here today."

"That makes two of us."

"Maybe, I thought there was some speck of motherly instinct inside of you but that's impossible when everything about you is bitter and hateful. Did you ever think that I left because of how horrible you were to me?

You criticized me relentlessly, hit me when you were drunk, and told me I was worthless. But after all these years away from you, do you know what I realized?

I didn't stop you from living your life. You stopped yourself. You could have still gone to college, had a career, loved my father as he deserved. It was never my fault. The reason you don't have anything or anyone is that you are a nasty, mean person. It is no one else's fault but your own!"

Renee pushed a tendril of hair from her forehead and raised her chin to the air in smug indifference.

"You have controlled me for far too long. I'm going to have this baby and I'm going to give it everything you never did. I will love and cherish it. I will comfort them in their pain and rejoice in their success. But most importantly, they will never know you."

Olivia stood from the couch with one hand on her stomach and the other pointing at her mother, "With God's help and encouragement from my wonderful husband, whom you chose to have nothing to do with, I forgave you. And I forgive you for this. But I refuse to let you hurt me anymore. I thought I could make this right but I was wrong. Goodbye, Mom. Someday, I hope you find God as I have."

Before Renee could spit one more venomous word at her, Olivia took a last glance around the house in which she was raised and walked out the front door.

The hour drive back to her and Grey's home felt like an eternity as she held back tears that threatened to spill from the deepest recesses of her soul.

When she pulled into the driveway, Liam and Diana's car was no longer there. As she unlocked the front door, her heart sank when she realized Grey wasn't there either. The garage was empty and the house was silent.

Instead of calling him, Olivia chose to take a hot shower to wash away the chill running through her numb body.

She went through the motions of undressing herself and stepping into the shower. Yet, as soon as the hot water ran over her body, she dropped to her knees under the running showerhead.

Let it out. Rid yourself of her oppressive grasp.

Twenty minutes must have passed as Olivia shook violently with sobs, a mixture of water and tears pouring down her face. Suddenly, the shower curtain pulled open and Grey's hands were on her back, "Oh my gosh. Are you okay? Liv?"

Olivia couldn't control the gasps of air her body now demanded as she nodded her head. Grey shut the water off and went in search of a dry towel from the cabinets under the sink.

When he returned, he covered Olivia with the plush cotton and wrapped his arms around her. Grey swiftly picked her up from the shower floor and walked her into their bedroom. He sat her on the edge of the bed and dried her off, "Breathe, Liv, breathe."

Once she was dry, he grabbed one of his t-shirts and a pair of sweats, helping her dress before pulling the covers back on the bed. She crawled up the mattress and lay under the warm comforter, breathing in the scent of Grey as her body still attempted to calm down.

"I'm so sorry I wasn't here when you got home. You didn't take as long as I thought you would. I figured I had time to go to the store. We ran out of milk and eggs."

Olivia welcomed Grey's warmth as he crawled under the covers next to her. His arms wrapped around her waist as he curved his body around hers. Her throat was raw when she finally spoke, "It's okay."

"You should have called me or, better yet, I should have gone with you."

"No, this was something I needed to do alone."

It was quiet for a minute as Grey traced his fingers along her still flat stomach. His lips and warm breath skimmed against her neck as he held her tightly to his body, "Did you get what you wanted?"

Olivia contemplated his question before giving her indecisive answer, "Yes and no."

Though she would never have the mother she desperately wanted all of her life, she did receive something she needed that day: closure.

Chapter Twenty-Three

The following day, Olivia sat in her dad's backyard and watched as Grey and his parents effortlessly maintained a meaningful conversation. After yesterday, she was anything but sociable during the celebratory barbeque at Ellis's house.

Ellis and Audrey stood by Grey as he turned the steaks on the grill. Diana and Liam watched the process close by with interested expressions. Maybe being interested in their child's hobbies was just something good parents did.

Her dad clapped Grey on the back before retreating from the grill and taking a seat next to Olivia. They sat in silence for a few minutes, watching as Grey kept an eye on the grill while his parents and Audrey organized the picnic table for their meal.

"I assume it didn't go well with your mother."

Olivia shook her head and focused on the cuticle around her ring finger, fighting the stinging in her eyes.

"I figured as much. Sometimes there are people in your life who are cancerous. When you have a tumor, you have to cut it out. But I am sorry, sis."

It doesn't make the cut hurt any less.

"It's not your fault, Dad."

"In a way, it is. I had countless opportunities to take you away from her. At first, I thought her behavior was a phase, a shock to having a baby so young. When I realized it wasn't going away, I thought staying with your mom was best for you. Then, it hit me that I didn't want to spend the rest of my life miserable and I left. But I didn't just leave her, I left you."

"Dad, we've talked about this. It's okay."

Ellis swallowed hard and pushed forward in the conversation, "No, it's not okay. I should have fought for you. It shouldn't have mattered that you would've switched schools or moved away from your friends. My

238

decision to leave you resulted in harsher abuse. I was selfishly focused on my own escape that I didn't consider how staying with her would affect you. I said it would get better… but it got so much worse. I didn't know, Liv."

"I know, Dad. At the time, I didn't understand. But I do now. And I forgive you. I forgave you years ago."

"I see how much impact she still has on you. It's evident even in the little things like how you still put forks on top of plates in the sink as she demanded. And I know it's my fault. I can't help but think about what your life would be like if I would have just taken a stand against her."

Olivia looked up at Grey with his parents and then back down to her stomach. As if by instinct, her hands laid over her abdomen.

"If you had taken me away, I wouldn't have Grey. I wouldn't have a best friend like Morgan or in-laws who love me like they do. I wouldn't have this life inside of me. But, Dad, most of all, I wouldn't have God. It was in the worst time of my life that I realized how much I needed Him."

A tear escaped down Ellis's cheek as he smiled at his daughter. He reached over the arms of their lawn chairs and enveloped her hand in his, rubbing his rough thumb against her smooth skin.

"So, you don't need to apologize, Dad. Because I don't need to forgive you. I need to thank you."

The shock was apparent in Ellis's expression as his grip on her hand tightened, "Please, don't thank me for failing you."

"People make mistakes. But sometimes, if we work hard at it, we can make our mistakes into something really beautiful. Something worth the years we waited."

Olivia gestured at their small family with her hand before it rested back on her stomach, "And this, this was worth the wait."

Every second.

Olivia braced herself as the transition between memories continued to quicken. In less than a second, nine months had passed.

"I still feel like we're forgetting something. Grey, can you check the hospital bag again?"

She cupped the underneath of her bulging belly as she waddled into the baby's nursery. Grey followed close behind and guided her to the rocking chair in the corner.

"I've checked it three times, Liv. We have everything we need."

"I just can't fight the feeling that we're forgetting something. And my pregnancy brain isn't helping. Today, I put the milk in the cabinet with the cups."

Grey chuckled and knelt on his knees in front of his very pregnant wife. He placed his hands on either side of her stomach and pressed his lips on the protruding bump.

"I know you're nervous, honey, but everything is going to be okay."

"You can't possibly know that for sure."

"Very soon, I will have a beautiful baby girl in my arms and a gorgeous wife by my side."

"Grey, I need you to listen and don't stop me. Please, just let me say this. I need you to know."

"Know what?"

"If something were to happen to me during the delivery, don't hold it against her, Grey. When you look at her, don't think about what you lost by having her. Love her as you've loved me. And never, *never* let her think that my death was her fault."

Grey's voice was shaky as he interrupted her, "Liv, please, don't…"

"Listen to me, Grey. If something happens to me, tell her that I would have done it a million times over again for her. And that I love her *so* much."

A million times is still too small of a number.

Tears streamed down Grey's face as he nodded in agreement. He kissed her belly again before standing and pressing his lips on Olivia's forehead.

"Everything is going to be okay."

His voice had changed. When he spoke, it was not merely in reassurance but as if he needed to hear it.

Later that night, Olivia woke up with severe contractions. She reached over to Grey and shook his shoulder to wake him.

"Grey, I'm in labor. The contractions are really…"

She sucked in air as she attempted to breathe through the contractions tightening her stomach.

"Okay, okay. Let me know when you have another. I'll time them. Are you able to get dressed?"

Olivia nodded her head and grabbed a pair of sweat pants she had thrown on the dresser. Grey dressed and then left the bedroom to retrieve their hospital bags. With the bags next to the front door, Olivia and Grey sat on the couch and timed her contractions.

When it was time to leave for the hospital, Olivia stood in the middle of her daughter's nursery and breathed in the light, sweet scent of newborn laundry detergent. Grey unknowingly stood at the door, watching his wife with uncloaked fear in his eyes.

"Are you ready?"

As another contraction tightened Olivia's stomach, she gripped onto the side of the crib, breathing rhythmically. Grey supported her with a hand on the small of her back.

Suddenly, Olivia's memories fast-forwarded through the next few hours of her life: the car ride, the laboring in the hospital room, and the doctor arriving for the delivery.

Wait, God. Let me enjoy the last moments with Grey before it's over.

There was no pause before her final memory replayed. Again, she witnessed her daughter being taken from her chest and Grey yelling her name desperately.

However, this time, her memory expanded to watch as her own body was wheeled out of the room. Grey was attempting to follow his unconscious wife when a nurse stopped him.

"Where are you taking my wife? Please save her. I can't do this without her. Please, you have to do something. Let me be with her."

Grey! I'm here! Grey!

The nurse remained calm as she explained that Olivia had lost too much blood and was still losing it at an alarming rate, "She's being taken into surgery to find the cause of the bleeding. Once we find the cause, we can treat the problem. We are doing everything we can for your wife, sir. I'll be back with an update as soon as possible."

Grey was left alone in the room with the nurse and his newborn daughter, looking utterly broken. He painstakingly turned his attention to his daughter with the promise he had given his wife pressing on his heart.

Chapter Twenty-Four

Olivia was once again surrounded by complete darkness as the silence of her mind weighed heavy around her.

Why, God? Why would you make me watch my life again if I'm dying? What does it change now?

Though her voice filled the empty void, there was no answer. Instead, a soft, incandescent light shot against a wall of the void like a projector in a theatre.

She saw visions of her father from her life. Ellis looked so young as he held his newborn daughter in his arms, eyes bright with adoration. When six-year-old Olivia fell from her bicycle, her father ran to scoop her up from the ground and dry her tears.

Olivia watched as countless visions of her father played on the screen, all memories of her life on earth. He was there on birthdays and Christmases, graduations and sports events. Every scene before her led to the last time she saw her dad.

There was a moment when the screen was blank before it began the same process again, the soft glow flickering into images. However, this time the memories were filled with her grandmother.

Olivia's chest tightened when her eyes landed on her grandmother from the time of her birth to sitting in the pew at church, and, finally, to her funeral.

God, please.

Unrelenting, another slide show began with memories of Grey: when they were introduced at the church next to Vi, fighting on the beach, kissing on their honeymoon night, and putting together their daughter's nursery.

Finally, there on the screen were flashes of her daughter. At first, she was covered in blood, crying as she was put onto Olivia's chest. Then, she lay quietly in her father's arms waiting to hear the news about her mother.

When the scenes flickered away, Olivia dropped to her knees in surrender. Tears streamed down her face as she searched her pitch-black surroundings for an answer.

God, I don't know what you want from me.

The visions flickered back on the wall but now, they lacked the emphasis on a specific loved one. Instead, it focused on Olivia. It showed crying and laughing, failures and triumphs, hurting and celebrating, wins and losses.

And just like that, Olivia finally understood what God was trying to show her.

It's a message. You've been trying to communicate with me all this time. You've given me many loves: my grandma, my dad, Grey, and my daughter. Through them, you were showing your love for me, God.

The visions of her life played faster still, the flicker of light flashing across her face.

I see it now, Lord. The love you have for me. Grey told me about it but I couldn't understand until now.

Visions of her daughter filled the screen and she collapsed on her face overwhelmed.

It took having my daughter to understand that love. That unconditional, reckless, unrelenting love. You look at me like I look at her: beautiful, perfectly imperfect, and worthy of so much love.

I understand now, God. You've been with me the whole time. Through the hills and valleys of my life. In the waiting and the searching for answers. In the sleepless nights and hopelessness. In the losses and the victories. When I felt like I had no one. Every moment of my life, you were there.

The screen had gone blank following the last scene of her life. Her surroundings grew brighter as she began to hear sounds and voices close by.

Grey's deep voice was right beside her, "Hey, Liv. You did it, baby. You lost too much blood but they found the problem. You're going to be fine now."

His voice broke as if only half believing his statement. When a moment of silence passed, Olivia heard the soft cooing of her daughter nearby.

"Our daughter is right here. She has your gorgeous eyes and my nose. Liv, she's perfect. Six pounds, eleven ounces, nineteen-and-a-half inches long. I can't wait for you to see her."

Olivia felt Grey's hand on hers as she gradually gained consciousness. She welcomed the warmth of his touch on her skin.

"Your dad, Audrey, and my parents are in the waiting room. And Morgan is on her way. They'll be able to see you when we leave the recovery room. But, first, I know you'll want to hold our daughter."

Grey's lips pressed against her forehead, a teardrop falling on her cheek from his face, "I love you so much, Liv. I need you to pull through. She needs a mama who loves her like only you can."

I understand, God. It's so clear now.

Olivia's surroundings grew brighter as the hospital recovery room became more and more visible. Out of the corner of her fluttering eyes, she could make out Grey's figure with a small pink bundle in his arms.

My entire life has been a love letter from You. Every moment is evidence of your love for me, a new way to demonstrate your presence. I couldn't see it then, but I do now.

It's a letter I will read for the rest of my life, one I will share with my daughter and her daughter. A never-ending message of Your love for me. For us.

As Olivia's eyes fully opened to the bright fluorescent lights of the hospital room, she read the message inscribed on the ceiling, the first words of God's love letter written just for her. And it all began with:

Dear Daughter

ALSO BY KASSANDRA GARRISON:

The Influencers

The Legacy: The Influencers Book 2

The Walls We Built

Distant Stars

CONNECT ONLINE:

www.kassandragarrison.com

Instagram @kgarrison_books

Facebook @kgarrison.author

Goodreads

CPSIA information can be obtained
at www.ICGtesting.com
Printed in the USA
LVHW040254210323
742062LV00004B/30

9 798986 124735